As ever I am grateful for not only tolerating ... ... encouragement I am not sure I would have finished this book.

Chapter 1

Tom, or Thomas, as his parents always called him, was an average fifteen year old boy. He would be sixteen in six months time. He hated being called Thomas and the only people who were allowed to were his parents, them justifying this by telling him that's what they put on his birth certificate.

He was not academic. Preferring to play football, or any other sport for that matter, and meeting up with people of the opposite sex, this was his latest pastime. He failed his eleven plus exam which would have got him into grammar school and, surprisingly, passed an exam when he was thirteen which got him into a technical college. This was in

Tottenham, a suburb of London, and the college focused on the building industry, teaching bricklaying, plumbing, carpentry and all trades associated. Tom had been there a little over two years and hated it.

One evening he came home from college and announced to his parents that he wanted to leave school. He told them that a lot of his friends were already working and earning money and he was wasting his time there.

It would be an understatement to say that his parents were not happy, especially his father who was quite a disciplinarian. His father asked him what he planned to do, as if he wanted to leave school he would have to work. Tom hadn't thought this through and said he was not sure. His mother, who

worked in a factory making suits   in those

days most suits were made to measure   said

that because Tom was artistic he could get a job in the factory she worked in as a cutter and designer. Offering another suggestion, she said Tom's cousin was a hairdresser and perhaps he could get Tom a job as a hairdresser.

Tom thought about this. He did not fancy working in a factory, but he did know his cousin Stephen was always seen with good looking ladies and always had a nice car. He asked his mother to contact Stephen to see if there was an opportunity for work.

Tom's mother contacted Stephen who agreed to pick Tom up the following Monday at eight o clock and to take him to the salon to see what Tom thought. Tom spent the weekend dreaming of all of the beautiful girls he would meet.

At eight o clock on the Monday, Tom walked to the end of his road and Stephen stopped his car when he saw him. Stephen had the roof of his car down, dark glasses on and Tom thought, this could be me soon. Tom got in the car and thanked Stephen for the opportunity.

When they were driving to Golders Green, this is where the salon was, Stephen said, "They do not call me Stephen, I use the name Raphael, sort of stage name".

"I will remember," Tom said, "promise".

Thirty minutes later they arrived at the salon. It was a small salon called 'Hair by Margaret'. They both entered and Stephen introduced Tom to Margaret. Margaret was in her mid-thirties, slim and petite and had a warm smile.

She said to Tom, "Hello, come and have a seat over here" gesturing to some seats in the back of the salon.

"Thank you," Tom said and followed her.

"Tell me a little bit about yourself," Margaret said when they were seated.

Tom did not know what to say, he didn't think anything about him was interesting. He told her a little bit about school, not much to tell, and he told her his mother thought he was artistic and this might be good for him. Margaret seemed happy with his answer.

"We can take you on as an apprentice, the apprenticeship is for three years. Your starting salary will be one pound and twenty pence a week, it goes up every year, and you will have Saturday afternoons and Sundays off. How does that sound to you, Tom?"

Tom had nothing to compare this too so he said, "That will be fine. When can I start?"

"Now," said Margaret.

Tom's jobs were to sweep the hair from the floor, keep the salon tidy, clean the work stations and tidy the staff room. As well as this, one of the girls who was a third year apprentice trained Tom to shampoo. He also had the pleasure of making coffees for the clients and occasionally he would get tips for this.

After three weeks Tom was given his first client to shampoo. She was a very old lady with lots of grey hair. Tom welcomed her from the reception area and asked her to take a seat at the backwash. When she was seated she took off her wig and only had a few hairs on her head. Tom was horrified and the staff hiding watched and laughed.

Tom decided to treat her had as if she had hair and gave her two shampoos as normal. He then wrapped her head in a towel and escorted her to a work station. He then got his first tip, six pennies.

This went on for three months and Tom could see no advancement so he started to buy a *Hairdressers Journal* and looked for another job. He knew that to be successful you had to work in central London. There was an advert for an apprentice for a salon in Mayfair, the very posh part of London, and Tom telephoned asking for an interview. He was told to be there on Wednesday at two o clock to meet Mr. Mac, the owner.

Tom arrived five minutes before two o clock and went to the reception. A pretty lady looked up and smiled.

"How may I help you?" she asked.

"I am here for an interview with Mr. Mac," Tom answered.

The receptionist told Tom take a seat. She then picked up the phone, said something and then spoke to Tom.

"Mr. Mac will be with you shortly."

Five minutes later a man approached Tom. He was portly with thinning hair. He sat next to Tom and said, "Hello, Tom".

He held his hand out for Tom to shake it.

"Hello, Mr. Mac", Tom responded and shook his hand.

"Tell me, Tom, why should I employ you?"

Tom quickly responded.

"Because I want to be a great hairdresser and I know I will be a great employee".

Tom had rehearsed this response many times. Mr. Mac smiled. He then asked Tom where he was working, how long he had been there and did he have to give notice to his present employer.

"I have no formal arrangement with them but I would like to give then one week's notice. I think that is fair".

Mr. Mac liked that answer.

"Give your notice in this weekend and come and join us on Monday a week. Bring your National Insurance number."

With that Mr. Mac got up and said "Goodbye. See you soon". And left.

Tom had told Margaret that he was ill on Wednesday which is why he was not at work. When Tom went to work on Thursday

Margaret asked if he was feeling better and he said he was. He also felt guilty for the lie.

On the following Friday Tom told Margaret he wanted to leave, he apologised and said he would give one week's notice. Margaret was not unhappy, actually she was quite relieved because for the last month Tom's work was not good and she was thinking about telling him to go.

"No problem, Tom," she said to him, "I wish you luck. Collect your wages next Friday and you can have the Saturday off".

Tom thanked her and went back to work.

Chapter 2

On the Monday he was due to start his new job Tom left his house at seven thirty. He got a bus at the end of his road to take him to the tube station. The ride to Green Park, this was the nearest station to the salon, took thirty five minutes and the walk from there took five minutes. He arrived at the salon at eight twenty.

When Tom entered the salon Mr. Mac was seated at the reception desk looking at the appointment book. He looked up as Tom entered and smiled.

"Good morning, Tom. Have a seat there, please".

Mr. Mac pointed to the velvet settee that he sat on when he came for his interview.

"Good morning Mr. Mac", said Tom politely and sat down.

Mr. Mac spoke into a microphone that was on the desk and his message came out of speakers around the salon.

"Would Christina please come to the reception".

Within thirty seconds a young lady came to the reception. She was about eighteen years old, wore very strong glasses and was wearing a uniform, similar to the ones Tom's dentist wore.

"Tom, this is Christina," Mr. Mac said, looking at Tom. "She is the senior apprentice here, her three years are almost complete. She will give you a tour of the salon and show you where things are."

He then looked at Christina and asked, "Would that be okay?"

"Certainly, Mr. Mac," Christina said and then looked at Tom.

"Hello, Tom. If you follow me I will show you around."

She left to enter the salon and Tom followed.

The salon was so different to Margaret's. It can only be described as elegant. The walls were covered in heavy flock paper and everything was pristine. Tom noticed that there was a client sitting at one of the work station and a stylist was working on her hair.

In front of the client was a silver tray with coffee and biscuits on it. The salon looked like an elegant throw back of twenty year ago. Christina took Tom down some stairs and told him, this is where the staff room and the stock cupboards were.

After the tour Tom went to work. It was similar to the work he did at Margaret's', sweeping the floor, making coffee and keeping the salon tidy. On Tom's third day he was tested to see if he could do a proper shampoo and he passed this with flying colours. Over the next two weeks Tom was given some clients to shampoo, the tips were very good in comparison to the occasional tip he got at Margaret's. Clients here were allowed to choose who they wanted to wash their hair so Tom only got those clients that had not requested another apprentice.

After Tom had been there for two weeks, Christina approached him.

"How are you enjoying working here?"

"I like it very much," replied Tom. "Just one problem. Half the clients here are deaf and keep asking me to repeat myself."

Christina smiled.

"The clients are not deaf, they don't understand you. You speak too quickly and you don't finish your words. Also, there is no such word as 'nuffink', it is 'nothing'".

She said this speaking very slowly and succinctly. She then added. "Tom, this is not a criticism. I just want to help you to get on".

Tom thanked her and she left.

This gave Tom 'food for thought'. He had never thought of himself as being ambitious, but he now knew he wanted very badly to succeed. He promised himself that he would improve and he started to slow his speech down by half what it was before. He finished every word as if this word was the most important thing. On his tube ride home he bought *The Evening Standard* and started to do the junior crosswords. Finally, he bought a dictionary and learnt a new word every two days. These words were used, even out of context, at every opportunity. As an example, one day his word was 'palatial' (like a palace), but Tom would use it to describe a shop.

After being there for six months and realizing that the clients were not deaf, Tom had his own clientele for shampooing and he found he could live just on his tips. Over the next year Tom was taught how to apply hair colour, how to perm (Permanent wave) and there were lessons in dressing hair. Tom knew, it would be a long road to success. After the three years apprenticeship he would have to do two more years as an 'improver' before he could be considered a stylist.

Mr. Mac had a daughter, her name was Helga. She was eighteen and she joined the salon ten months after Tom. It became obvious to Tom that Helga quite liked him and they would tease each other at every opportunity. This was a time of the Miners strike and often in the day the power would be cut and the salon put into darkness. It was during these periods that Tom and Helga would sneak off to the stock room for a kissing and cuddling session. They were extremely careful as Tom knew he would be fired if caught.

Thirteen months into his employment Mr. Mac told Tom he wanted to speak to him. When they went down to Mr. Mac's office he told Tom to have a seat.

"Tom," he said, "I am going to let you go. You can have one week's notice".

Tom was shocked.

"Is my work not good enough?"

"Your work is fine, but I think you are too friendly with young ladies. You can have any time off for future interviews."

There was never a reference to Helga, but Tom suspected somebody had seen them and reported this to Mr. Mac.

Tom was back to buying the *Hairdresser Journal* and job hunting.

Using the money he had saved, mainly his salary, as he lived on his tips, and a bit of help from his father, Tom bought an old Mini car which broke down every time it rained. He had passed his driving test soon after he was seventeen. Tom's father was doing quite well as he now had two large contracts and five men working for him.

One job he saw advertised was a salon in Crawford Street, close to Baker Street station. He arranged, by telephone, an interview with Mr. Rupert, this was the same name as the salon, for Thursday at midday.

Tom got the tube to Baker Street and found Crawford Street, which was only a five minute walk from the station. He was ten minutes early for his interview, but he walked into the salon. This salon was so different from Mr. Mac's, so modern with a small reception area and only three work stations in view.

The man sitting at the reception desk was in a smart suit, double cuffed shirt and probably in his thirties. He looked up as Tom walked in and said, "Are you Tom?"

"Yes, I am. Are you Mr. Rupert?"

"Yes," said the man. "Tell me about your work to date".

Tom told him about his three months in Golders Green and his time in Mayfair. Mr. Rupert asked him why he wanted to leave Mayfair and Tom told a little lie, saying he wanted to find a salon that was doing more modern work. Mr. Rupert liked his response and asked when he could start.

"I have permission to start as soon as I can find another job," Tom said.

"Start next Monday," Mr. Rupert said. "It will be a three months trial and we shall see how we get on."

"Okay," Tom said. "That will be great. Thank you."

The following Monday Tom arrived at Baker Street station soon after eight thirty, he didn't want to be late. He was at the salon five minutes later, but the door was still locked and it was obvious that there was nobody there. He decided to have a walk around the area and get back for eight fifty which he did. There were some lights on in the salon and the door was open.

Sitting at the reception desk was a very attractive young lady, probably around twenty five years old. She looked up when Tom entered and smiled.

"You must be Tom, the new apprentice," she said.

"Yes, I am," Tom replied.

"My name is Jessy, I am the receptionist here. Welcome, Tom".

"Thank you. Where should I go?"

"People here are not early starters. They should be here in the next ten minutes. Why don't you have a seat and wait for somebody to show you around."

Tom said thank you and sat down.

Ten minutes later Mr. Rupert entered, said hello to Jessy and Tom and then he went down some stairs. This seemed to open the flood gates as many more people came into the salon, saying hello to Jessy and nodding to Tom. Soon after nine o' clock Mr. Rupert came up the stairs with another young lady.

"This is Brenda," he said to Tom, "and she will show you around and introduce you to the rest of the gang."

Brenda smiled and said to Tom, "Come downstairs and I will show you the staffroom."

With that, she went downstairs and Tom followed. When Tom reached the bottom step he could see there was another salon here with eight work stations. They walked a little further and there was a door on the right and Brenda walked into this room. Several people were sitting drinking coffee, some were smoking.

They all said hi and Tom replied, hi. This was so different to Mr. Mac's, so casual and so laid back.

"Make yourself some coffee," Brenda said, "smoke if you like and, as the day wears on, I will introduce you to these lazy people."

All of the people smiled at the reference to 'lazy'. Tom made himself some instant coffee and sat down next to another young lady, she was about twenty five years old.

She looked at Tom and said, "Hello, my name is Joan. I am one of the stylists here."

Tom looked at her and said, "Hello. It is nice to meet you".

The last place that Tom worked previously was staid, serious and sedate as opposed to this place, which really represented what was to be known as 'the swinging sixty's'.

There was a message through a loudspeaker.

"Joan, your first client is here."

Joan drained what was left of her coffee and left. Tom was now sitting next to a man of similar age to Joan. He said to Tom, "Hi, my name is Dallas. I too am a stylist here."

"Hi," replied Tom.

As Dallas, he preferred this to 'hello'.

One by one the staff left the staff room leaving just Tom and Brenda there.

"Each stylist here has their own junior," Brenda said, "we don't use the word apprentice, and you have been allocated to help Joan. You will shampoo her clients and generally assist her. She works upstairs with Mr. Rupert and Dallas. Mr Arnold works down here. The best thing you can do for now is to go and join her and ask if you can help."

Tom smiled and said, "Okay, I will do that."

With that he went upstairs.

When Tom got upstairs he saw Joan was shampooing her client. He didn't want to interrupt her conversation so he waited in the background until she had finished shampooing. When she finished, she wrapped a towel over the client's head and moved her to a work station. Once the client was seated, Tom approached and asked Joan, "Can I help?"

Joan said to her client, "This is Tom and its' his first day. Tom, this is Mrs. Allbright and she has been my client for six years."

"Hello Tom," Mrs. Albright said. "I hope you enjoy working here. Joan is not only a great hairdresser but a lovely person."

Joan and Mrs. Albright smiled at Tom.

"I am going to set Mrs. Albright's hair," Joan said to Tom. "If you want, you can pass me the rollers and pins."

There was a trolley on wheels next to Joan which she wheeled towards Tom. Tom stood by the trolley and was ready to pass whatever Joan wanted.

Tom discovered that there were four stylists, including Mr. Rupert and four juniors and, of course, Jessy, the receptionist. The day passed quickly with Tom meeting the other juniors, they were all boys and occasionally talking to the other stylist. The atmosphere was so different from his last job and the clients were so much younger. Tom later found out that many were celebrities, married to famous people or just famous in their own right.

Stephen, the oldest junior, worked for Mr. Rupert. Lenny, who was the smallest junior worked for Dallas and Peter, the junior with the wild hair, worked for Mr. Arnold. Tom was happy to work for Joan as she was the most cheerful.

During his lunch break Tom was talking to Brenda in the staff room. She explained to him that every Tuesday, after the last client had left, there was a school night which each of the stylist took it in turn to preside over. She said, whispering, "The juniors prefer Joan to teach, they say she is the most fun. Mr. Arnold is the strictest and, from what I am told, Dallas just gets them started and then goes to the pub."

"Thank you for the information. I shall keep it in mind," said Tom, smiling.

That evening as Tom was going home Mr. Rupert approached him.

"Tom, every Tuesday we have a training session after work. I will not involve you tomorrow but, bear in mind, you will be expected to attend in the future. Good night."

"Good night," replied Tom.

And he went home.

On the way home he did the usual buying his *Evening Standard*. He had now progressed from the junior crossword to the adult one. He was feeling pretty pleased with his first day and was happy to have chosen Mr. Rupert's salon.

The rest of the week he got to know the other juniors and learnt how to cope better with the stylists. On the Saturday they were meant to finish by one o' clock, but was told this never happened. At one forty five the juniors were told they could go. Tom ran all the way to Baker Street station. A few stops later, at Kings Cross, he had to change train lines. Then he eventually arrived at Manor House and he ran out the exit. He jumped into a taxi with three other people after discussing with the taxi driver where they all want to go. Their destination was White Heart Lane, the home ground of Tottenhem Hotspurs, Tom's favorite football team.

He rushed in to try to get in before the kick off. His friends were all in the Paxton Road end and he made his way there to join them just as the whistle went to start the match. Spurs, as they were known, won and Tom went home happy.

On the Monday, other than a heated argument between Brenda and Dallas, nothing much happened. On the Tuesday after the last client had left, four young ladies walked into the salon, these would be the models for the training session with the juniors.

Mr. Arnold was to be their teacher. All models were gowned and sat down. This lesson was about perming (permanent wave), how to roll the hair around the perm curler, how to check it was ready to be neutralised. Neutralising makes the curl permanent.

The next two months followed a similar pattern. The only thing that was different was, Stephen, who was naturally clumsy, was shampooing one of Mr. Rupert's client's. Somebody spoke to him and he turned around and the water spray was straight into the client's face. This became the last straw for Mr. Rupert who immediately fired him. Mr. Rupert then told Joan, who was the last to be employed, that he would like to take Tom as his junior. She said that would be fine but would he employ somebody for her. Mr. Rupert said he would.

Chapter 3

Tom was enjoying his work and over the next few months very little changed. The only significant thing to happen to Tom was in his home life. He and his parents were living in a shared council house with Tom and his parents living on the ground floor and another family living upstairs. This meant that Tom's family did not have a bathroom, just a sink to wash in so once a week Tom's father would take him to the municipal baths to have a bath.

Tom's father had his own building firm, if it could be called that. There was only him and another employee whose name was Winkle because he had a glass eye. Harry, Tom's father, was a gambler, especially on horses. There was a family joke that he donated to sick horses but he didn't know they were sick until they lost the race.

Harry placed a lot of money on a horse named Santa Claus which won and Harry then had enough money for a deposit for their first house. They moved into a house in Tottenham and had their own bathroom as well as three bedrooms.

After Tom had been working at Mr. Rupert's for four months there was an incident in the salon. Mr. Rupert asked Tom to take his client, Mrs. Leicester, out of the dryer. Mrs. Leicester looked like she was asleep so Tom carefully lifted the hood of the dryer slowly so as not to frighten her. When he lifted the hood Mrs. Leicester looked like she was still asleep so Tom gently nudged her shoulder. She still didn't move so Tom called Brenda over. Brenda tried to shake Mrs. Leicester and then Brenda ran to the phone and called an ambulance.

The ambulance arrived within five minutes and the two paramedics picked up Mrs. Leicester and put her on a stretcher and carried her to the ambulance. Dallas, who thought he was a comedian said, "This is great publicity. Our promotional material will read. 'Come to Rupert's salon and dye'". Nobody laughed.

Two days later Mrs. Leicester walked in to the reception. Brenda was shocked and stuttered, "We thought you were…"

Before she finished her sentence Mrs. Leicester smiled and said, "I suffer from diabetes and go into shock. Once the put a drip in I was fine. Now, can I get an appointment to have my hair done please?"

Brenda said yes, looked at the appointment book and offered a time and date. Mrs. Leicester agreed and Brenda said, "I will have a bar of chocolate on the reception desk."

Tom worked at Mr. Rupert's for almost eighteen months but with all of these stylists having previously worked at Vidal Sassoon's he could see that he would not get a chance to go further. He likened it to being a graduate at a football team who would never get into the first team. He decided to leave.

He still wanted to stay in central and he got a job as an improver at a salon near Marble Arch. The salon's name was Mason Roderick. The owner told Tom to spend three months just watching the other stylists. There was one particular stylist that adopted Tom, his name was Michel. He was incredibly handsome, with dark skin and a sexy French accent. While he was doing their hair the clients just swooned. The problem was, Michel preferred men! He was kind to Tom,

noticing that Tom had not had lunch   Tom

was not getting tips so he could not afford sandwiches. Michel gave him his sandwiches.

Tom suggested to Michel that they go out together, maybe find some nice young ladies.

"Good idea," Tom responded, "not sure about the young lady bit, but come to my house for dinner."

Tom was not keen on this idea.

After three months of watching and not getting any tips, Tom decided to leave.

He handed in his notice and on his final day he went round to say goodbye to everyone. When it came to saying goodbye to Michel, Tom offered his hand for a handshake. Michel smiled.

"Are we not friends?"

"Of course we are," Tom said.

"Friends kiss goodbye," replied Michel.

Tom was confused, he felt guilty, as Michelle had been so kind, but he had never thought of kissing another man. Eventually he offered Michel his cheek.

"No, on the lips," Michel said.

Tom did not know what to do so he ran out of the salon.

Tom had seen an advert for a stylist in a salon in Shaftsbury Avenue, just off of Piccadilly Circus. Although Tom had not completed his two years improver course, he was now confident with his hairdressing and he now looked and acted older than his seventeen years, he would be eighteen in two months.

He telephoned in response to the advert and got an appointment for an interview on the Wednesday afternoon. The salon was called Mr. Leon. Tom felt a little guilty to pull a sick leave but had no option and he took the day off on Wednesday.

Tom arrived at Mr. Leon's salon at two o' clock and was interviewed by Mr. Leon. They talked for twenty minutes with Tom explaining how ambitious he was and giving Mr. Leon some idea of his past. Tom did some exaggerating of his achievements.

After talking Mr. Leon became silent whilst he was thinking and then said to Tom, "I have another idea for you, Tom. I have a small salon, which I tend to use as a school, and I want a manager there, do you think you could do it?"

Tom, with an air of bravado, said, "Yes, I am sure I could."

"When could you start?" Mr. Leon then asked.

"I have to give at least one week's notice and, If I do this at the end of this week, I can start on Monday a week," replied Tom.

Mr. Leon discussed salary, which was much, much more than he was now getting and agreed that Tom should start on the Monday. They shook hands and said their goodbyes and Tom left.

On Friday, Tom handed in his notice to the owner of Mason Roderick, who told him he could leave the following Friday and have the Saturday off.

On the Monday that Tom was to start at Mr. Leon salon he arrived at eight thirty. Mr. Leon was in the reception area and he approached Tom.

"Good morning, Tom. Come with me and I will show you where the salon is, it is only a two minute walk."

Tom followed Mr. Leon and while they were walking down Shaftsbury Avenue towards Piccadilly Circus Mr. Leon said, "Tom, I think it best if you tell people you are twenty because you will be managing the salon."

Tom said that he will do this.

They walked to for just two minutes, then turned left into Rupert Street. On the right was the salon. Mr. Leon entered and Tom followed.

The salon can only be described as a long room. On the right there were three work stations and opposite these there was a three banked drying section. At the rear of the salon there were two backwashes. When they entered, the staff came out of a door at the back and approached both Mr. Leon and Tom.

Mr. Leon was the first to speak.

"Good morning, this is Tom, your new manager."

The staff all nodded towards Tom. Mr. Leon then faced Tom and pointed towards the two people that were there.

"This is Barbara, she prefers to be called Babs, she is a stylist here, and this is Terry, he is a junior."

Tom turned towards them and said, "Good morning, I am sure we shall all work well together."

They both smiled and replied, "Good morning."

Mr. Leon left and Babs said to Tom, "Shall I show you the staff room?"

"Yes, please," Tom replied.

Babs walked to the room that both of them had come out of and entered, followed by Tom. The room contained two chairs and a table with an ashtray on it. There was no room for any other furniture.

"Would you like a coffee?" Babs said.

"Yes please, milk and no sugar. Tell me a little about the salon?"

Babs put the kettle on and got down from a cupboard on the wall two mugs.

"There really is little to tell. I have been here six months and we get an average of four clients a day, sometimes more but sometimes less."

Babs told Tom where she has worked before and conversation finished there. Tom thought he would have his work 'cut out' to make any success here.

As the weeks progressed Babs's summary of the situation became clear and when 'casual clients', ones that didn't have appointments, came in Tom took them. It was two months before Tom discovered any improvement and he was starting to get a bit of a reputation and some recommendations.

The clientele was young and a mixture of dancers from the local theatres, aspiring actresses who said 'they were resting', Tom discovered that this meant they were not working, and young ladies who worked at St Margaret's Place, a place that was well known to hire rooms for an hour.

One day, on Tom's birthday, Babs brought a cake in and put up a sign saying, "Happy Birthday, Tom!"

Tom had four clients booked in that day and one of them was a dancer who worked at The Pigalle theatre. She said to Tom, "Happy Birthday, Tom. How old are you?"

Tome was nineteen but had to keep up the lie so he said, "Twenty one."

The dancer arched her eyebrows.

"I thought you were older than that."

Tom didn't know whether to be pleased or insulted. He smiled.

"I have had a lot of late nights recently."

They both laughed.

A week after Tom's birthday he was doing one of his regular client, she worked at St Margaret's Place. It was fashionable to have your hair piled up on top and then put the hair that was left into curls. He finished her hair and she swore.

"Is there a problem?" Tom asked.

"I stupidly forgot I am wearing a rolled collar jumper, how can I get this off without spoiling my hair?"

Tom didn't have an answer but she smiled as if a Eureka answer and said to Tom, "I need you to cut the back of my jumper and I will wear my jacket until I get home."

She stood up.

"Right, cut right up the back."

Tom did this in the middle of the salon and the client went and put her jacket on, paid and left, leaving Tom a large tip.

After Tom had been there for five months, taking, although still low, had doubled. He went to Berwick Street market to buy some lunch for himself. One of the ladies which was a client, she worked at St Margaret's place, approached Tom.

"Hello Tom. I have a proposition for you."

Tom smiled.

"Tell me."

"My boyfriend has been with me for nine weeks, using the money that I earn, and he has just paid cash for a new sports car."

"That doesn't sound very fair, are you happy about this?"

"No I am not, how do you fancy taking his place?"

Tom was in shock. He thought if he did his father would kill him.

"That's a great offer," he replied, "can I think about it?"

"Yes, let me know. You know where to find me."

A month after this Mr. Leon came to the salon. He gathered all of the staff into the staff room and said, "I am sorry about this but I have just sold the salon, it is going to be a nail bar. You have two weeks to find another job, I wish you all luck."

With that he left and the three of them just looked at each other.

Chapter 4

Tom's next job was in a small salon in South Kensington. There was only the owner, one other stylist and one junior. He went to the interview and had to do a test shampoo and set. What Tom lacked in hairdressing skill he made up for with impish charm and flattery.

The work was okay, nothing special, but the social life in South Kensington was hectic. Lots of Australians lived in this area and there seemed to be a party every night. Some parties he went to he met people who were on their third consecutive party.

The people attending these parties were diverse. On one particular party he would spend an hour joking and talking to people working in the City. At the end of this evening he got talking to a young lady and when he asked her what she did for a living she told him she sold her body. Tom arched his eyebrow as if to say 'seriously'. She smiled and said 'yes'. Tom took her to her house at four in the morning and dropped her off there, saying goodnight.

This salon was nothing like the other salons he had worked in. It did not have the charisma or charm of Mr. Mac's and Mason Roderick and not the modernistic look of Mr. Rupert. He decided it was time to leave.

A friend of his worked in a salon in Winchmore Hill and he told Tom that they were looking for a stylist. Winchmore is an expensive suburb of London and Tom telephoned, using the number that his friend gave him, and arranged an interview on the Saturday afternoon. The salon in South Kensington closed at lunchtime so Tom did not need to lie and take time off.

He met the owner whose name was Tony at two o' clock and they chatted for an hour. Tony asked Tom when he could start and Tom told him he would like to give one week's notice to his present employers. They agreed on a salary and Tony told him to start on Monday a week.

Tom arrived at the Winchmore salon at eight thirty, he did not want to be late. He thought to himself how nice it was to have a twenty minute drive as opposed to the hour plus it took him to get the bus, then the tube to central London.

The salon was quite large and, although not ultra-modern, was nice. There were three other stylists plus Tony, the owner. The head stylist was a man in his early twenties, then there were two other female stylists, Lisa and Georgina, who used the name Georgie. As well as these people there were two apprentices named Gerry and Ann. They also had an older lady who made teas and coffee for the clients, she also helped with the cleaning, her name was Agnes.

Tom enjoyed the work there and the rest of the staff was good to work with. Within four months Tom had a good clientele and was really enjoying himself.

Tom had got together with his cousins, they were more friends than relations, and three of them, together with Tom had arranged a week's holiday in a holiday camp on the east coast. Tom was the only one to have a car but, not trusting its reliability, they decided to go by train.

Barry was the eldest of them and Harvey was six months older than Tom. Raymond was the youngest. Once they were at the camp they had two chalets, Raymond would share with Barry and Tom and Harvey would have the other one. They spent their time getting involved with the activities, playing football, all of the other sports and whatever activities were on offer.

On the third day Tom got friendly with a young lady and they spent quite a bit of time together, her name was Julie. On the last night there, Tom went to Julie's chalet and he fell asleep there, but was woken at six in the morning by a message over the tannoy system telling him to return to his chalet. He was angry thinking his cousins were playing a joke on him.

When he arrived at the row where his chalet was he saw his father's car was parked outside. He sheepishly went in and said to his father, "Good morning."

His father was quite gruff.

"You had better get packed."

Tom packed in silence, his cousins had already packed and they all got into Tom's father's car. On the journey home Tom fell asleep for most of it.

When they arrived at Tom's house the first thing he noticed was his car was not there.

"Where is my car?" he asked.

His father smiled and handed him some keys and then nodded to a brand new Ford Anglia.

"I think you should take your cousins home."

With that he went into the house leaving Tom just staring at the car. His cousins smiled because they knew about the car as Tom's father had told them while Tom was asleep.

Tom enjoyed his time in the Winchmore Hill salon but a new twist happened soon after his twentieth birthday. Tom's grandmother's second marriage was to a man that was well off. He died a few years into their marriage.

Soon after Tom's birthday she died leaving money and the property to Tom's father and his brother Ben. Uncle Ben, as Tom knew him, and his father did not get on and there was some argument as to how to share the inheritance. Tom did not know what sum was involved or how the argument was sorted out.

Three months later Tom's father told him that he had seen a hair salon for sale in the same area and the salon had a nice flat above the shop.

"Would you like to have your own salon?" he asked Tom.

"Yes please," said Tom.

That was the start of Tom's Hair Salon!

Chapter 5

Tom's father did all of the negotiations and it was agreed that Tom would work there for three months before they signed the agreement. The salon, at the moment, was called Rory's, which was the present owner's name. Tom gave his notice to his present employers and went the following Monday to work with Rory.

Tom and Rory got on really well, they even had the same taste for the opposite sex which created a healthy competition. The staff that worked there were Brenda, she was the senior stylist, Janice, who was the improver, and the junior named Melanie who preferred to be called 'Mel'.

After three months, contracts were signed and Rory left. As this salon was not too far from Tom's old salon, some of his clients came to him and things went well. Tom told his clients a new joke every week, the staff got fed up from hearing them, but for the clients it was the first time that they had heard them.

The flat above was quite large and had two bedrooms, a large lounge and dining room with a kitchen and a bathroom. The whole family moved in.

Tom bought himself an open top sports car and he was becoming a personality around the Winchmore Hill area. Things were going well for two and a half years, then everything changed.

There was an empty shop opposite the salon which Tom's father signed the lease for. He planned to make this into a dry cleaning shop for himself and Tom's mother.

Tom's parents decided to take a break and go to Mallorca for a week and Tom agreed to use his father's car (his was being repaired) and collect them from the airport on their return.

On their first day in Mallorca Tom's father telephoned and asked Tom to call a number (which he gave him) and to tell the young lady on the other end of the phone that her mother had arrived safely. Tom called this young lady, her name was Jessica, and passed the message. Tom liked her voice and suggested that they meet for a coffee. She agreed and Tom said he would call again to make arrangements.

On the Sunday that they returned Tom went to collect them and when arriving at Gatwick discovered that their plane had been diverted to Luton Airport. He drove as quickly as possible but it was still two hours later he arrived.

Tom's father was not too happy and the journey home was made in silence. When they got home Tom apologised and his father relaxed saying it was not Tom's fault.

Tom was on the committee of a charity that made money for a hospital in Jerusalem and they were running a dance that night to raise money. Tom, being on the committee was expected to go. He told this to his father and his father smiled and threw his car keys at Tom. Tom went to the dance.

When Tom got home soon after one o' clock he noticed the lights on in the flat. His first thought was 'I am twenty two and they still wait up for me'. He let himself into the flat and noticed the kitchen light was on so he went in there. Sitting there was Tom's mother and two friends, Lucy and Maurice. Maurice stood up and went to Tom and put his arms round Tom.

"I am sorry, Tom, your father is dead. He had a heart attack."

Tom pushed Maurice away.

"You're lying. It's not true."

Tom then broke down and cried. When his tears had stopped he looked up and said, "Where is he?"

"He is upstairs in the bedroom," Maurice said. "He didn't suffer, it was very quick".

Tom's family were Jewish and, although they did not keep up the religion very strongly, they kept with the traditions. When somebody dies a family member has to stay with the body throughout the night, this probably stretched back to days of body snatchers. Tom knew, as the son, it was his job to do this. Before he went upstairs he telephoned his best friend, Harvey, and told him what had happened. Harvey said he would come immediately.

Tom went upstairs and into the bedroom. His father was on the bed covered from head to toe in a sheet. Tom just sat on the floor and sobbed. Forty minutes later Harvey arrived and both the boys spent the night in the bedroom. Several times Tom thought he saw his father move.

The next morning all of the family arrived and Tom's uncles organized the funeral. It is a tradition in Judaism that the body should be buried within three days (probably something to do with being in the desert) and this, with the help of the family, was achieved. There was one incident when the rabbi approached Tom to offer his condolences.

Tom angrily said to him, "The bible said we should live three score year and ten. That's seventy years. My father was fifty seven. What happened?"

"Somebody else will get the years that your father has lost," the rabbi said.

Tom spent some time hating anybody over seventy believing that they were using his father's years.

Another Jewish tradition is that close family, son, daughter husband or wife, have to sit in mourning for seven days. This is called Sitting Shiva. During those seven days family and friends would come, some bringing cakes, and pay their respects. Prayers were said every night and Tom had to do the main prayer.

On the third day of sitting Shiva Tom was about to learn a lesson he would never forget. Brenda came up from the salon and said to Tom, "There is a not very nice man in the reception, swearing and wanting to see you."

"Did you tell him what had happened and that I must not enter work?"

"Yes, but this did not stop him, I am sorry, Tom, but I do not know what to do."

Tom sighed.

"Okay, I will come down."

The man was in the reception and approached Tom, threateningly.

"Where is my money for repairing your car?"

Tom tried to placate the man.

"Because of my father death's I am not allowed to do any form of business. If you come back in four days I will pay you."

The man screamed.

"I don't give a f..k about your dad. If you do not pay me now I will smash in your window."

There were a few more swear words. Tom told Brenda to take the money out of the till which she did. The man snatched the money out of her hand and stormed out. Tom then thought, so, that's what life is about.

Once all of the services were over Tom looked at all situations. The money situation was not great and there was not enough money to completely open the dry cleaners shop, this being a priority as they were already paying rent.

Tom decided that it would be easier for him to get work so he decided that he would sell his salon and complete the dry cleaning shop. He put the salon in the hands of an agent that specialised in hairdressing salons. In the meantime he called Jessica and they made a date to meet at a coffee place they both knew.

They met at the shop in Willesdon and had coffee and they did not stop talking, Tom found out that Jessica was an actress and had already been in a couple of plays on the television. They arranged to meet again the following week.

It had been three months since Tom had given the agency the salon to sell and he had heard nothing. During that time Tom and Jessica had become close and decided to marry. The ceremony was held at Caxton Hall, by Jessica's request, she said all of the celebrities got married there. The party was at Jessica's flat with thirty people attending. Tom and Jessica were then going to her mother's place in Mallorca for their honeymoon.

Her mother had an apartment on the third floor of a private block. Tom hated heights and it took him three days before he would go out on the balcony. They met many nice people, but Tom got on well with a man named Maurice Cohen, who had two estate agencies.

When Tom returned home there was no news about the sale of his salon. He decided that he would put an advert in the *Hairdressers Journal*, which he did. He had seventeen replies and within a few weeks agreed a sale.

Now Tom had a problem, what to do for work. He didn't fancy being a hairdresser working for somebody else, but he did have an idea. He got a good response from his advert and he contacted Maurice Cohen and asked him what he thought about going into that business. Maurice said he thought it was a good idea and he did not have a commercial department.

"I have a spare office and I could put in a phone line for you, do you fancy trying it out?"

Tom said yes and they arranged to meet.

The following day Tom met Maurice at one of his offices which was in Eastcote. The office was a medium size with a desk to the left and another to the right as you walked in. Further down the office on the right was another small office with a glass door. Maurice ushered Tom into this office and they sat either side of the desk that was in there.

Maurice asked Tom what he had been doing and Tom gave him an outline of his career to date.

"What does your wife do for work?" Maurice asked Tom.

"She is an actress, but not working at the moment."

Maurice was curious and asked, "When was her last part she had?"

Tom felt a little uncomfortable answering.

"I think it was about three years ago."

Maurice frowned but didn't think it was his place to make a comment.

Maurice was like an older brother or even a father figure and had sympathy for Tom. They discussed their financial arrangement and it was agreed that they should have a partnership in the commercial business. Maurice would help Tom financially with a loan and this would be settled at the end of the year when they shared the profits. Maurice also said if needed, he had a car that he didn't use and Tom could use it if he wanted. Tom thanked him and said he would like the use of the car as opening the dry cleaning shop was becoming more expensive that he thought and this would allow him to sell his sports car to help with the financing. After two hours of conversation they shook hands and Tom left.

Tom, who was now living in Jessy's flat, went home and told Jessy the news. She was pleased.

"I can now tell my friends that my husband is in real estate."

Tom was a little confused because he wasn't, but it seemed to make her happy, so he said nothing.

Over the next week Tom sold his car and arranged the 'finishing touches' to opening the dry cleaners shop. He spoke on the phone to Maurice daily to update him with his progress and Maurice told him to use public transport to get to Eastcote on Monday and then he can have the VW Beetle to use.

On Monday morning Tom took the tube to Eastcote and arrived at the office at eight thirty. Maurice took him into the office where they had had their chat and told Tom that this was his office. He had installed another telephone line which would be solely for the commercial business. He handed Tom three folders and said that these were the only commercial businesses he had, they were all shops for sale. Maurice left him to study them.

Tom could see that the most important thing for him to get on with was to get more businesses and later that day he spoke to Maurice about this.

Maurice said, "We could try some 'Charlie' adds."

Tom was puzzled.

"What are 'Charlie' adds?"

Maurice smiled.

"We put an advert in saying 'JP is looking for a tobacco shop with or without accommodation.' You follow up any responses and try to get them on our books".

Tom thought that was a great idea and Maurice said he will place the advert. After the add came out there were three replies and Tom agreed with the owners that he will come and see if their business was what JP wanted.

Tom arrived at the address of the business. There was no name, just a sign that said 'news and tobacco'. Tom opened the door and a bell rang and he saw a man standing behind the counter. The man looked up.

"Can I help you?"

"My name is Mr. Levy," said Tom, "we have an appointment regarding your business."

The man smiled, he had been trying to sell his business for quite some time.

"Well, this is the shop and if you would like I can show you my accounts for the last three years."

Tom said that would be great and the man left. Tom took some pictures of the shop and the man returned with a set of accounts. He handed Tom the accounts.

"If it makes it easier for you, I do not need the account at the moment and you can take them back to your office to study them," the man said.

"That's' a good idea. I will be in touch with you in the next two days," replied Tom and then left armed with the accounts.

Tom also went to the other two people that had replied to the advert and followed the same process. Two days later he telephoned the first shop he went to and said to the owner, "Your shop is nice, but unfortunately it is not what JP was looking for. Would you like to put your business on our books and I will try to find you a buyer?"

The man, although disappointed, said yes. This was Tom's first success.

After the first two months, although there were no pending sales, Tom had twenty seven businesses on his books. Financially, things were difficult. He couldn't ask his mother for help as the business had only just started and he had to rely on the loan arrangement he had with Maurice.

Three months later Tom decided that the situation was serious. Jessica was still not working and, as much as he wanted to tell her she had to make an effort, he couldn't bring himself to do it. He came up with a plan to tell her he would have to take a second job and, hopefully this will inspire her to go and look for some sort of work to help out.

When he got home that night he sat down to have a talk to Jessica.

"We are not managing with our money situation so I think I will have to take a second job in the evening after I finish at the office."

Jessica looked surprised.

"What will I do when you are working in the evening?" she said.

Tom was shocked, this was not the response he was expecting. He shrugged.

"This cannot be helped. We have no options."

That night, Tom lay in bed awake thinking his wife had disappointed him. It was the start of their breakup.

Tom applied for a barman's job in a pub in Hampstead called 'The Old Bull and Bush' and got the job. For the next two months he finished work at the office and drove straight to the pub and finished work there soon after eleven o clock. Then it was home a sleep.

He then decided that he didn't want to be married to Jessica, he was starting to even dislike her. Determined to leave he chose the following Thursday to put his plan in action. Jessica had a long standing friend named Clive and Tom and Clive played chess together. Tom telephoned Clive to tell him of his plan to leave and explained that he did not want to leave her alone after he told her he was leaving. It was arranged that Clive would come to the flat at a time that Tom had finished speaking to Jessica.

Chapter 6

Tom had preplanned all of this including finding a room in Harrow, paying a deposit and telling the landlord which day he would be moving in.

On the following Monday Tom had arranged with the pub to have a night off. This was going to be the night of the separation. He had kept Maurice informed of his plan,

Maurice was secretly happy because he didn't like the way that Jessica treated Tom, and Maurice loaned him a suitcase.

When Tom arrived home he put the suitcase down and Jessica, looking surprised asked, "What is the case for?"

Tom, having rehearsed to himself, replied, "It is for my clothes, I need some time alone."

Jessica was shocked.

"Why?"

Tom was expecting this question.

"I think that I have not got over my father's death and I need to be alone to come to grips with this."

Then the doorbell rang. Tom knew who it was so he went to open the door. Clive walked as if nothing was going on and saw Jessica in tears. He went to comfort her.

"What's wrong?"

In between sobs Jessica said, pointing at Tom, "He's leaving me."

As agreed, Clive turned round to Tom and said, "I think you should leave."

Tom nodded, packed his things and left.

Tom found a telephone box and called his friend Harvey. Harvey said he would meet Tom at the Old Bull and Bush within the next hour. Tom drove to the pub. Arriving at the pub, for Tom there was a sense of relief that 'the deed' was done and it was nice to see some friendly faces of the staff that he got on well with. Tom wasn't a drinker but he ordered a vodka and lime. He had three more and, not being used to drinking started to feel a little drunk.

Thirty minutes later Harvey came in to the pub, saw Tom and joined him. Tom told him how it went and Harvey was relieved that Tom was okay. Harvey said he would drive Tom to his room and he would have to sort out how to get his car back the next day.

The next couple of weeks went by and while he was at the office he received a call from Jessica. She was quite pleasant, asking how he was and how he was managing. He said he was fine and 'working through' things. Then Jessica surprised Tom.

"I have been to see a rabbi and he wants to see us both. Would you agree to this?"

Tom really didn't know what to say but he said, "Yes."

She told him where the synagogue was and when to be there. He agreed to this and it was to be the following Monday evening.

Tom told the landlord of the pub that he would be a little late that day and the landlord said it would be fine.

On the Monday evening Tom arrived at the synagogue at six thirty, Jessica was already there. They said hello to each other just before the rabbi came out to greet them.

The rabbi said, "Hello, my name is rabbi Levy and I believe that the two of you are having difficulties."

Both Tom and Jessica nodded. The rabbi continued.

"So, let's all talk."

Tom was first to speak.

"If we are going to talk I would like us to do it separately."

Tom knew he could never be honest with Jessica in attendance. "That's fine," the rabbi said. "Let's start with you, Tom. Come into my office."

He walked to the back of the synagogue and Tom followed. When they were in the rabbi's office and seated, the rabbi said, "Tell me the problem."

Tom told him the whole story including telling Jessica about his father because he did not want to hurt her more than she already was. The rabbi listened intently and, at the end of Tom's story, the rabbi nodded.

They went back to join Jessica and the rabbi asked her to follow him to the office. They were only gone for ten minutes and both Jessica and the rabbi came back to where Tom was sitting. The rabbi addressed both of them.

"I cannot help you. Your joint problem will have to be sorted out between you and it will take whatever time it takes. Sorry."

Jessica was devastated. She was hoping that the rabbi would suggest that Tom was having a breakdown and that was the cause of their breakup.

Three weeks later Tom received a letter which was sent to the office. It was from a solicitor acting on behalf of Jessica demanding that Tom pay Jessica alimony. Tom was not sure what to do. He spoke to Maurice and he could not offer a suggestion.

Tom knew that the sales going through his half share would be enough to pay Maurice back but how would he survive the following year if he had to pay alimony. As well as the sales going through they still had seventy three businesses on their books but each sale took a long time.

He made a decision to leave Maurice and go and find a job. He spoke to Maurice about this who was disappointed but understood. Tom remembered one of the people who wanted to buy his salon had twelve other shops. The only reason that Tom did not sell to him was he wanted Tom to remain at the shop and be in his employ. Tom telephoned him and said he was looking for work. Anthony, the owner of the company, told Tom to come and see him and he will find a place for him to work. Anthony knew what Tom was capable of.

With what little money that was left over after he paid Maurice back, Tom bought a very old car. He drove to Welwyn Garden

City to meet Anthony. Anthony was at the reception when Tom arrived and ushered Tom to the back of the salon to a small office.

When they were both seated Anthony said, "Do you mind where you work?"

Tom replied, needing the money, "No."

Anthony said that Tom could work here as a senior stylist until a managers' job came up. They discussed salary and it was agreed that Tom would start the following Monday.

The following Monday Tom arrived at the salon and, sitting behind the reception desk was a pretty young lady. She smiled when Tom walked in.

"Do you have an appointment?" she asked.

"No, I am here to work," Tom replied smiling back.

The receptionist smiled again and said, "You must be Tom. I was told to expect you. My name is Greta and I will tell the manager that you are here."

She left the reception desk and walked to the back of the salon to the office where Tom had spoken to Anthony. When she came out of the office she was accompanied by a man who looked like he was in his early thirties. He was quite tall and walked with a limp. He walked directly towards Tom and put his hand out to be shaken. Tom shook his hand.

"Hello, Tom, and welcome. My name is Gregory, I am the manager here." He then smiled and said, "Not sure the rest of this lot believe it."

Tom and Gregory both laughed.

Gregory took Tom around the salon and introduced him to the rest of the staff and showed Tom what would be his work station.

Over the next two days Tom got to know the names of the other staff. There was Leonard, the other senior stylist, this was also Tom's title and Jill, who was a stylist and had been there for six months. Also there was Ruby who was a first year improver and two juniors named Toby and Jessy.

Business for Tom was slow as he was only given new clients, ones that did not mind who did their hair. The staff were all nice and, apart from not being busy, Tom was happy. The other bad side to not being busy was, there was very little in the way of getting tips.

Three months after Tom started in Welwyn Garden City, Anthony came to the salon. Once he had spoken to Gregory in the office, he called Tom to the office to join them. Tom went in and sat in the only available chair.

Anthony was the first to speak. He said, looking at Tom, "How would you like to go to Grantham?"

"Where is Grantham?" Tom replied.

Anthony smiled.

"It is about one hour up the A1."

Tom smiled back.

"You have a Rolls Royce, it could take three days in my car."

Both men laughed. Then Anthony said, "There is a salon there which I want you to manage. Grantham is a small market town and, if you worked at it, you could become some sort of celebrity there."

Tom thought for a moment and thought he had nothing to lose so he said, "Yes, that will be interesting."

Anthony spoke to him about pay, it was not much more than he was already receiving, and told Tom to meet him at the small airfield in Mill Hill saying they would fly up to Grantham in his plane. This was arranged for the following Monday, four days from now.

On the Monday Tom arrived at the airfield. Tom was embarrassed to park his battered old car in the car park as all of the cars parked there were very expensive. As Tom got out of his car Anthony approached.

"Hi, follow me."

They made their way out to a runway and parked there was a Cessna two seater plane. Tom stood there staring and remembering his fear of heights.

Anthony went around the plane doing various checks.

"Probably the most important thing in flying. Not a good idea to have the engine stop."

He laughed at his own joke. Tom just forced a smile. Once the checks were complete they both got into the cockpit, Tom sitting next to Anthony. Anthony gave him a set of earphones so he could listen to any communication, and Tom put them on.

The plane taxied to a runway, stopped and then accelerated down the runway. Within seconds they were in the sky. By this time all of the blood had drained from Tom's face and he did not think he had ever been so scared. Anthony saw Tom's fear and chatted away. He told Tom that even if the engines stopped they could glide the plane down, that's how gliders do it. He said the only real danger was hitting telephone wires.

After thirty five minutes they started to descend. Anthony told Tom that he had an arrangement with a local farmer to use his field to land in. It was just outside Grantham in a village called Stroxton. From there Anthony would get a taxi into town. They descended onto the field, it was a bit bumpy, but Tom had lost most of his fear. After taxiing toward some buildings they stopped fifty yards before they reached them.

An old looking man came out of one on the buildings and walked towards Anthony. They both shook hands and spoke far enough away that Tom could not hear what was said.

Ten minutes later a taxi arrived and Tom and Anthony got in. Anthony told the driver where to go and off they set. Ten minutes later they were in the centre of the town. They entered the salon, Tom noticed the name on the outside, Anthony Hair Fashion, and all there was to see was a reception desk with some retail product on shelves behind the receptionist.

"Hello, Mr. Anthony," said the receptionist, deferentially.

"Hello, Lisa," Anthony replied.

Then he turned and went up some stairs, followed by Tom.

When they got to the top of the stairs the space opened up to show eight work stations, three backwashes and a drying bank consisting of six dryers. Two of the work stations were occupied with clients sitting in the chair and hairdressers standing behind them and two of the dryers were being used as well.

"Hello, Mr. Anthony," all of the staff said in unison.

Anthony smiled and nodded his greeting.

One by one they came to be introduced to Tom, it was a case of if you are not busy, come and meet your new manager. First to come was Janet who said, "Hello Mr. Tom, I have been here for three years."

Tom said hello back.

Next was Brenda and the same thing happened with Brenda referring to Tom as Mr. Tom. She was followed by one of the juniors, the juniors wore different aprons, Joanne, and the same hellos were said. She was followed by Tess, the other junior.

Finally, when she was free, as she seemed to be the busiest, Theresa came to meet Tom. Tom was first to say, "Hello." Theresa replied, "Hello, I am Theresa, I have been here twelve years. I hope you like Grantham."

Every once in a while the speakers in the salon would call out somebody's name to say 'your client is here'. There was a small microphone in the salon so you could speak to Lisa, the receptionist. After being there for two hours Anthony spoke to the microphone and asked Lisa to order him a taxi to go to

Stroxton. They both said goodbye to all of the staff and made their way downstairs.

When Tom and Anthony got in the taxi Tom was marginally less fearful of the flight back.

After two weeks, Tom had given notice to his rented room and he packed his things into his old car. The drive to Grantham didn't take three days but it did take two and a half hours. When he got there he checked in to the cheapest hotel he could find and the first thing on his agenda was to find somewhere to rent.

He went to a newsagent and bought a local paper to look for 'accommodation to rent'. One advert he liked was an old cottage on the outskirts of town in a village named Little Gonnerby.

He went to the salon, said hi to Lisa and asked if he could use the phone.

"Of course, you are the boss now."

She was smiling.

Tom thanked her and rang the number to try to rent the cottage. The lady that answered had a strong Lincolnshire accent and just said, "Hello."

"Do you still have the cottage to rent?" asked Tom.

The lady sounded surprised that anybody was interested in it and said, "Yes, I do."

"Is it possible I could see it?"

"Yes," the lady said and they agreed to meet at the cottage in the next hour. She gave Tom the address and directions of how to find it.

Tom went to the newsagents and bought a map of the area so he could familiarised himself. He then set off to Great Gonnerby to see the cottage. He found the cottage easily, the village was very small and the cottage was just off the main road. He parked his old car and saw a lady standing outside. Tom approached and smiled, the lady smiled back.

"I spoke to you an hour ago about renting the cottage. My name is Tom and I am the new manager of Anthony Hair Fashion."

The lady seemed quite happy to have 'middle management' renting her property.

"Hello. My name is Mrs. Brooks. Would you like to look inside?"

Tom said yes and Mrs. Brooks, using a key, opened the front door.

When Tom walked in he couldn't believe his eyes. This property, being in Grantham, was costing the same as Tom had paid for his rented room. There was a small kitchen to the right and a huge lounge with a dining table and four chairs at the back. On the left was a very large Inglenook fireplace which you could almost walk into. Tom went up the stairs and there was one larger bedroom, could just about be call a double, and one smaller bedroom, definitely a single, and a bathroom which was adequate.

"I would like to take it. What are the terms of payment?"

Mrs. Brooks did not want to lose Tom so she said, "Normally I charge a month's deposit but I will not charge you. If you pay me the rent at the end of each month I will be happy. Is that Okay?"

"That will be fine. How soon can I move in?"

"Whenever you want," Mrs. Brooks said.
"Tomorrow?"

Tom was so happy, no more paying for hotel.

"That will be great. Thank you."

Mrs. Brooks handed Tom the keys.

"I hope you will be happy in Grantham."

She then left.

The next morning at the salon Tom called for a staff meeting. When they were all assemble Tom said, pointing at Lisa, "I am Tom and you are Lisa. So, no more Mr. Tom. We are a team and all trying to be successful."

The staff all smiled and nodded agreement.

Chapter 7

The next few months the salon carried on a usual with no great success but no backward steps. Tom was enjoying his life in Grantham and he also enjoyed the relationship with his staff. He was doing less hairdressing but more motivation and management. There were times when he had to learn a different language. When he told his local shopkeeper he landed in a field in Stroxton the shopkeeper looked puzzled. Tom tried to explain where this was and the shopkeeper smiled.

"You mean 'Stroson'," he said, even though it was spelt like Stroxton.

Another incident was when he asked one of his staff to get him a ham roll. She asked whether he wanted a 'cob' or a 'bap', Tom did not know what she was talking about and told her to choose. He later discovered a 'cob' was shaped like a ball and a 'bap' was larger and flatter.

Three months later Tom was shocked when his friend, Harvey, turned up at the salon. Tom took Harvey to a nearby café for a coffee and a talk.

"Great to see you," said Tom. "Has anything happened?"

Harvey looked a little shaken up.

"It is better for me to be away from London at the moment. Do you mind if I stay with you for a little bit?"

Tom knew Harvey did not gamble so that could be not be the problem. He also knew that Harvey was not good with money and was fired as a shoe shop manager for money missing. It seemed obvious that Harvey did not want to talk about it so Tom did not press the questioning of why Harvey should be out of London.

"Of course you can stay with me. I have a small two bedroomed cottage just outside town. When I finish work I will show it to you."

Harvey told Tom he would have a walk around the town and come back to the salon at five o clock. Tom then went back to work.

At closing time Tom went down to the reception and saw Harvey in deep conversation with Lisa. Tom told Harvey he was ready to go and after both of them said goodbye to Lisa they went to find Tom's car. When they arrived at the cottage Tom opened the door and ushered Harvey in. Harvey looked around.

"This looks lovely."

Tom smiled. He then showed Harvey where everything was kept and showed him the bedroom that he didn't use.

"You can have this room," he said to Harvey.

"Thanks," said Harvey.

Two months after Harvey moved in he still had not found work Worse than that, he didn't even look for work, but made full use of the account with a taxi company that Tom set up for him. Tom thought to himself that this was like living with Jessica but Tom was a loyal friend so he said nothing.

One evening Tom and Harvey went to the cinema. Sitting behind them were two young ladies. Harvey, who was far more forthright than Tom, turned to the girls and asked them if they would like to go for a drink after the film. The girls looked at each other and the girl that was the slimmest said yes.

At the end of the film they all walked out, Tom and Harvey were out first so they waited for the girls to come out, which, within a minute, they did. The girls approached the boys and the one that agreed to go for a drink said, "Hello, my name is Elizabeth but I prefer Liz."

She then turned to the other girl.

"This is my friend, Annette."

They all shook hands and Harvey said, "My name is Harvey and this is Tom. Shall we go to *The George Hotel* for a drink?"

They all agreed and *The George Hotel* was a three minute walk.

Once they were all seated Harvey asked the girl what they would like to drink. Liz asked for a small lager and Annette said she would have the same. He then asked Tom what he would like and Tom said a vodka and bitter lemon. Harvey looked at Tom with a little desperation and said, "Shall I get the drinks or do you want to?"

Tom knew that Harvey had no money so he said, "I will" and Tom went to the bar to order the drinks.

When Tom brought the drinks back to the table Harvey asked, "What do you, girls, do for work?"

Liz, who was seated next to Tom, said, "I am a receptionist at an opticians and Annette works in the factory just outside town which makes shoes."

"What do you men do?" Annette then asked.

Tom told them he was the manager of a hair salon and they all looked at Harvey.

"I have only just got here so I haven't found a job yet," said Harvey.

Both Harvey and Tom knew this was a lie. The four of them chatted away for an hour, with Tom buying a second round of drinks. Liz asked where they lived and Tom told her about the cottage.

"If you guys would like," Liz said, "we can come to your cottage and cook you a Sunday roast."

"That would be great. We can send a taxi to pick you up," said Harvey.

The girls said for the taxi to collect them at eleven thirty and they would buy the food adding, looking at Harvey who appeared to be the main man, "You can buy the drinks, and I don't mean lager. A couple of bottles of wine will be good."

Harvey nodded and said, "No problem."

The girls wrote down the address for the taxi to pick them up and then said 'see you on Sunday'.

Tom and Harvey then walked to the car, Tom was angry, but said nothing. When they got home Tom poured himself a drink, vodka and bitter lemon, and Harvey poured himself a large Brandy which he had asked Tom two days ago to buy. Tom decided it was time for them to have a talk.

He looked at Harvey and said, "Where is the money coming from, I spent quite a lot at *The George*, I now have to buy two bottles of wine, not cheap stuff, how much is this going to cost me?"

Harvey looked sheepish. Eventually he replied.

"I will get a job, don't worry, I will help out."

On the Saturday Tom bought some wine, one bottle of red and a bottle of white. Harvey did some cleaning and in the evening they played some cards.

On the Sunday morning Tom telephoned the taxi company and gave them the address to pick up the girls. He told the taxi company to put the fare on his account. The girls arrived at eleven forty and when they came into the cottage, Liz went straight to Tom and gave him a cuddle and a peck on the cheek. Annette did the same for Harvey. It seemed like the girls had decided who should be with who.

Tom's relationship ended after four months. They wanted different things, she marriage and, after Jessica, Tom was not keen on this. Harvey's relationship with Annette carried on and Annette found out she was pregnant. After they had been together for just over a year their son was born, they named him Damion.

Harvey found a part time job in a bookmaker's, his salary nearly covering his cab fares to get there. When Damion was two months old Annette and Harvey split up, she had found another man so Harvey was a full time father. One night, Harvey sat down and said to Tom, "There is assisted passage to Israel to migrate there and I am thinking of using it and taking Damion with me. What do you think?"

Tom didn't really know what to say but said, "If you think that is best for the both of you, go. Your opportunities here are not great. What will you need?"

"The fare money to get me back to London," said Harvey. "When I get there I will stay with my parents who are keen to see Damion and make arrangements to emigrate while I am there."

Tom secretly was relieved, Harvey was costing him a lot of money.

"I can give you the train fare to London and a little extra for travel from the train station if that will help."

Harvey thanked him and one week later, Harvey and Damion were gone.

A week later two bad things happened to Tom. Firstly, the landlady, Mrs. Brooks, told Tom that she was selling the cottage and he would have to find something else. Then the following day Anthony telephoned to say that his company were moving in a different direction and he was going to sell the salon to a perfume company and this would take place in the next two to three weeks.

"You can come back here and work in Welling Garden City until I can find you a management position," Anthony said. "Can I

have a couple of days to think about this?"
asked Tom.

Anthony said yes and the conversation was
over.

That night, Tom was deep in thought. He did
not want to go back to Welling Garden City
as he liked it here in Grantham. There were a
number of salons in Grantham but only three
of any worth. One was a salon named Mario
Hair Fashion, this was part of a chain of five
salons. Another was a salon named 'Curl up
and dye', this was owned by a lady who was
known not to be nice to her staff. The third
salon was called Gerrards, this was only
recently opened.

Although Tom had no reputation as a
hairdresser he had become well known
around town. He decided that he would go to
Mario and see if they wanted a stylist. After
his salon closed that evening he walked to
Mario's, it was less than three minutes, and
walked in. There was a young lady at the

reception, she looked up at Tom and asked, "How may I help you?"

"I am enquiring whether you want another hair stylist," replied Tom.

"Take a seat and I will get Sergio, he is the manager."

With that she got up and went into the salon. A minute later a man who had a Mediterranean look and was about the same age as Tom came into the reception area. He walked up to Tom and put his hand out to be shaken.

"Hello, I am Sergio and the manager here. I know who you are, Tom, is that correct?"

Tom smiled.

"Yes."

"Have you come to spy on us?" said Sergio, still smiling.

Tom laughed.

"No. I am looking for work."

Sergio looked surprised.

"What about the salon you manage now?"

Tom told him about the company's plans to sell the premises, he told him he was offered a job, but didn't want to leave Grantham.

Tom and Sergio chatted for a while. Sergio said that Tom should work here but he did not have the space for the rest of Tom's staff. He also said that his uncle owned the company and he was based in Leicester. Tom gave Sergio a brief resume of what he had done and both men got on well.

They discussed salary and commission and they both agreed that Tom would start on Monday a week. When the conversation was over both men shook hands and Tom left. Tom's only regret was for his staff, but he did not know how to solve this. He decided the next day he would speak to them to give them as much time as possible to find work.

The next day Tom told Lisa to make sure there was an hour when they had no clients and told her to lock the door and to instruct all of the staff that there would be a meeting in the salon for everyone. Lisa said that there was a blank hour (no clients) at eleven o clock. Tom said this was fine.

At eleven o' clock all of the staff were gathered in the main salon. Tom stood where everyone could see him. He told them about the company's plans and said they had just under two weeks to find another job. Fortunately, they should have no problem finding another job as there was a shortage of juniors and the stylist will be able to offer their clients to whatever salon they went to. This made Tom feel a little better.

Tom now had to find somewhere to live. Through playing bridge at the local club, it had become quite a passion of Tom's, he knew Terry, the person that employed Harvey. They got talking and Terry said he had a small flat in Barrowby Road. He offered it to Tom and the rent turned out to be the same as the cottage. Tom was to move in the day after the salon was closed, a Saturday.

On their last day in the salon, Tom bought some fizzy wine and the girls bought some things to eat. They all toasted each other and Janet stood up and said, "I personally want to thank you, Tom, you have been a good manager and fun to work with. I wish you luck."

With that, all of the staff stood, raised their glasses to Tom, and said, "To Tom." This bought a little lump to Tom's throat.

Chapter 8

The next day Tom was to move into the flat that Terry had offered to him. Tom met Terry at eleven o' clock, as arranged, and gave Tom the keys. The flat was in walking distance of the salon. It was small, with one bedroom, a lounge, kitchen and bathroom. Tom unpacked his things and started feeling better about his future.

At nine o' clock on the Monday morning Tom went to Mario's. Sergio greeted him at the reception and he had booked out one hour to introduce Tom to the rest of the staff. They went up some stairs and there was another salon there. Sitting in one of the seats was another man with a Mediterranean look. He stood up and approached Sergio and Tom. He held out his hand for Tom to shake.

"Hi, my name is Gianni, short for Giovani. Welcome to our mad house."

The three of them chatted for a while and Gianni told Tom he came to England three years ago. He said he could not speak a word of English but, knowing Mario, he knew he had a job to come to. He had to use mainly sign language to speak to the clients but he managed. At ten o' clock somebody called from downstairs that Gianni's first client had arrived and was coming upstairs. Tom and Sergio said goodbye and they went downstairs.

The next person that Sergio introduced to Tom was Colleen, a junior stylist. Tom had already met Colleen as she was the girl who he saw when he first came to the salon. They shook hand and spoke for a few minutes with Colleen telling Tom that she had been working there for two years already. Sergio took Tom around the salon and introduced him to the other two members of staff, both juniors, Paul and Jenny.

At this point Sergio's first client came into the salon and he organized for one of the juniors to shampoo her. Tom didn't have any clients that day but had two the following day. After three weeks Tom was doing about fifteen clients a week. His number was growing every week.

Tom kept in regular touch with Maurice, he was like an older brother and Tom always felt he was looking over him to make sure he was fine. One day, while in the salon, Tom received a telegram. All that was written on the telegram was, 'are you dead?' Tom smiled, this could only come from one person, Maurice. It was his sense of humour. As soon as he had some spare time he telephoned Maurice for a catch up.

Tom had been in Grantham close on to three years. He had made many friends through the bridge club, although the average age of the bridge club was about sixty, through his local pub and though a lot of clients. One weekend one of his clients invited him to a party. Tom bought a bottle of wine to take to the party and arrived at the client's house soon after eight o clock.

Tom knocked on the door and his client, the hostess, answered the door and welcomed Tom. Her name was Vicky.

"Come on in," she said, "you will know most of the people and those that you don't, you will get to know them."

Tom gave her the wine and went in. Vicky was quite right, Tom did know most of the people there.

At nine o' clock Tom saw a lady he had not seen before. He approached her and said, "Hi, my name is Tom."

She smiled back.

"Hello, my name is Jenny."

She had an interesting voice which Tom thought was somewhere in the north of England. They started a conversation with Jenny telling Tom that she lived in Leeds and was just down visiting her friend Vicky. She also said she was married. They spoke for two hours and obviously liked each other. As the party died down Jenny agreed to go to Tom's flat for a drink. She did this and stayed the night.

Jenny and Tom kept in touch by telephone every other day. Two weeks later Jenny said she could come down for the weekend if he would like. Tom told her this would be great and they made arrangements to meet on the Saturday.

On the Saturday that Jenny came to visit Tom took her to a restaurant in the evening. They talked most of the night and Jenny told Tom that she had four children, the eldest being twelve, the next one being eleven, the third being eight and the youngest being five. If she tried to shock Tom she failed. They had a lazy Sunday together and then Jenny had to return to Leeds.

The following Tuesday Tom got a phone call from Jenny. She was obviously upset and Tom asked her what the problem was. "I told you when we last met that my husband and I do not get on. That was fine, not speaking etc. Now he is getting violent and I am scared."

Tom could feel the fear in her voice.

"Why don't you leave him?" he said.

"Where could I go," said Jenny, between sobs, "I have four children."

"Come here," said Tom, without really thinking this through.

Jenny stopped crying.

"Do you mean it?"

Tom felt he had committed himself and said, "Of course."

The conversation ended and three days later Jenny turned up in a taxi with four children and a dog. Tom paid the taxi twenty pounds and ushered everyone into his small flat.

Jenny introduced Tom too the children. The eldest was named Ruth, after that the second eldest was Joanne, the third, Becky, and the youngest was named Saul. Tom had no idea where everyone would sleep, but Jenny seemed to take charge of this and ordered children where they would sleep.

Two children slept in Tom's bedroom, on a mattress on the floor, two slept in the lounge, on armchairs. The dog slept in the kitchen. To say it was crowded would be an understatement. Tom was friendly with the young couple that lived in the flat above and Tom spoke to them after two days. The young couple took pity on Tom and, although they thought he was mad, they agreed to exchange flats, their flat having two bedrooms. They made this exchange over the weekend and Tom bought them a bottle of the most expensive brandy he could find as a 'thank you'.

Over the next three months a routine was established. The whole family would watch their favorite programme, *Poldark*, then they would read a few chapters of *The Hobbit* before the children were put to bed

Tom was doing well at work. His clientele had grown and he was now doing as many clients as Gianni and Sergio. Tom's workstation was upstairs which is where Gianni worked. They all got on pretty well, but Tom could not understand the Italian attitude. One day Gianni and Tom had a furious argument. Tom was fuming. At the end of the day Gianni said to Tom, "How about we go out and have a drink when we finish before you get inundated with children?"

Gianni laughed at his own joke and Tom just shook his head in disbelief, thinking, this guy is crazy.

"In spite of you being an idiot, you can buy," said Tom.

They both laughed and went for their drinks.

Two days after this Tom was in the salon feeling very tired. He sat in the drying bank and almost fell asleep. When it was time to go home, Tom's walk to the flat, which was normally four minutes, took him almost fifteen minutes. It was like walking in water with the tide going against you. Every step was hard work.

He eventually got home and with the aid of the railings on the stairs, managed to get to their flat.

Jenny saw him at the top of the stairs and he looked like he was about to fall back down. She ran to him and grabbed his arm and led him into the lounge. His face was very red and he was burning up. She managed to help him into the bedroom and into bed.

They had made friends with a doctor, through the doctor's wife being a client of Tom's. Jenny telephoned Bob, the doctor, and told him about Tom. He said he would be there within five minutes. When Bob arrived Jenny took him to the bedroom where Tom was. He examined him and told Jenny that Tom had a severe case of flu. He told her that Tom must not have food until the fever broke and she was to make sure he had the medicine that Bob had prescribed. All she could do other than that was to let Tom rest.

Tom shivered for two days and sweated profusely. On the third day he tried to get out of bed but his legs gave way and Jenny had to help him back into bed. On the third day Tom's fever broke and Jenny soon fed him some soup. He improved day by day and on the fifth day he got out of bed and walked to the kitchen. It took Tom almost three weeks to fully recover because, through the illness, he had lost so much weight.

Four months later, one evening Tom went home and Jenny was excited. She said she had heard of a house for rent and the rent was not much more than they were already paying. It was an old farmhouse and had four bedrooms. Tom told her to go and see the landlord to discuss the situation with him.

Two days later, when Tom got home, Jenny was really excited. She told Tom that the landlord had accepted her and they could move in the Saturday after next.

On the Saturday of the move they all piled everything into Tom's old car. The dog had to jump onto the three children that were sitting in the back, but the drive would only take three to four minutes. They drove on the Barrowby Road away from town and just before they reached the turn off to the A1 (the major road to London and the North) there was what can only be described as a dirt track, to the right. Tom drove up this track for almost half a mile and they the saw the house on the right.

The house was huge and there was not a neighbor in sight. Tom parked the car and everybody got out excited to see their new home. They walked in through the back door into a massive kitchen and dining room. The dining table could easily have fitted ten people around it. The kitchen had a double AGA and when this was lighted it would heat the whole house. Walking from the kitchen, on the right, was a very large lounge and on the left was another, smaller lounge. They all went upstairs to see the four bedrooms and the family bathroom. Jenny took charge and told each child which bedroom would be theirs.

They all unpacked and settled in for the night. Tom had packed the television so they had their usual routine. *Poldark* and then *The Hobbit* before the children were sent to bed in their new home.

Life went on quite well until one night. Tom saw a car coming towards the house up the dirt track and wondered who it could be. The car parked outside the house and two policemen got out. They came to the front door and knocked. Tom went to the door and opened it.

"Are you Mr. Thomas Levy?" said the policeman that was standing closest to Tom said.

"Yes, I am," said Tom.

"Mr. Levy, I am arresting you for non-payment of your alimony and you will have to come with us."

Jenny heard this and ushered the children away from the door.

Tom said okay and the policemen ushered him to their car. They drove to Grantham station. Tom was then handcuffed. One of the policemen went to have a word with the porter there and then returned and said, "The next train to London will be in fifteen minutes. I have organized a carriage for us."

The three of them waited till the train arrived.

When the train arrived the three of them boarded it and found a separate carriage away from the public. As the train left the station one of the policemen un-cuffed Tom. They asked him what had happened and Tom told the story, how he forgot to pay and was now feeding a family of six, including himself. The policemen felt sorry for him.

After they had travelled for an hour Tom said he would like to use the toilet. One of the policemen said they would have to come with him.

"Inside?" Tom said jokingly.

The policeman smiled and said he would stand outside.

An hour later they arrived at Kings Cross station. Once the train had stopped one of the policemen approached Tom and said he was sorry. He showed Tom the handcuffs. Tom put his hands together and the cuffs were secured around his wrists.

The three of them walked out of the station and a police car was waiting there. The door was opened and Tom was told to get in. Tom didn't know where they were taking him but he later found out it was to Willesdon magistrates court. They drove down the side of the court and went into, what appeared to be an underground car park.

Tom got out of the car when it stopped and was taken by one of the policeman through three secured doors. He was then placed into a cell. It was a very large room with five of these cells around the walls. Three of them were occupied, but the people inside were asleep.

Tom didn't have his watch on because it was taken away from him, together with other items as he was 'booked in', but he imagined it to be around four in the morning. Tom just sat in his cell and couldn't believe what was happening. How could Jessica not work and cause such misery. He believed that when he told the judge he was supporting the family that had moved in with him and the alimony was a third of his salary, the judge would be sympathetic.

What appeared to be two hours later, one of the guards entered and put down to each of the occupied calls some food and something to drink. The other prisoners woke up and grabbed the food from the floor outside their cells.

Tom couldn't eat. The room became noisy with the other occupants talking to each other. It became clear to Tom that this was not their first visit here. Another three hours later a guard came and unlocked Tom's cell and Tom was taken up some stairs and into a court room.

Once Tom was put into a closed off area the Judge said, "Are you Thomas Levy?"

"Yes," Tom replied.

"Do you plead guilty to not paying maintenance to your former wife to the sum of one hundred and twenty four pounds?"

"Yes, but…"

That was as far as Tom got. The judge interrupted.

"I sentence you to six weeks in prison. Next case."

He then slammed his hammer on his desk. One of the guards collected Tom and took him back to his cell.

As the guard put Tom into his cell he told Tom he could have one phone call. Tom didn't know who to call, his mother was on holiday in Mallorca. He decided that he would call Maurice. Tom called to the guard and said he would like to make his phone call now please. The guard unlocked Tom's door and took him out of that room into a smaller room where there was a telephone attached to the wall. The guard pointed to the telephone and said he could use it.

With shaking hands, Tom rang the office and was put through to Maurice by Maurice's secretary. Tom told Maurice the story of what had happened and explained that in six hours he would be transported to the main prison. Maurice asked where Tom was and said, "Let me see what I can do."

Tom was taken back to his cell and just sat there. He had no idea of the time or how long it was since he had spoken to Maurice, it felt like hours. After some time, a prison guards came to Tom's cell and unlocked it.

"You are about to be released," he said, "come with me."

He was taken up some stairs and there was a large counter with another guards standing behind it. The guard handed him a brown paper bag.

"These are the items we took from you. If you could just sign this form you are then free to go."

Tom signed, collected his things and walked out to the street. Maurice was standing by his car waiting for him.

"Get in. I will take you to my flat."

The drive was mostly in silence as Tom was still in shock but as soon as Tom got in the car he said to Maurice, "Thank you, I am not sure what to say."

Maurice smiled and replied, "If you are not sure what to say, say nothing."

As he said this he gave Tom a fatherly squeeze on the shoulder.

They drove to a place in West London and round the back of some shops. They went up a set of iron stairs and Maurice pulled out a set of keys and opened one of the doors. Shock had just started to set in and Tom started to shake. Maurice put his arm around Tom and led him into the flat. He led him to an armchair and poured Tom a very large brandy and handed it to Tom.

"Drink that and I will organize a nice hot bath for you."

With that Maurice went into another room.

Tom looked around the flat and decided it was typical Maurice. All of the furniture was modern and expensive. After a few minutes Maurice came back into the room.

"Go in there and have a hot bath and we can talk more when you come out. There are towels hanging on the rail."

Tom went in, undressed and got into the bath. The combination of the brandy and the bath relaxed him. He soaked for five or ten minutes, got out of the bath and dried off. He then went back into the lounge.

Maurice was the first to speak.

"Your ex lazy wife is a cow."

They both smiled. Tom just nodded. Maurice continued with a smile on his face.

"That's the first time we have got together and you haven't made a joke."

With this even Tom laughed.

Chapter 9

After Tom had told him everything Maurice said, giving Tom some money, "This is enough for you to get a taxi to Kings Cross station and enough for your fare back to Grantham. I have to get back to the office so leave whenever you want to."

"I don't know how to thank you," Tom said to Maurice.

Maurice replied, again with a smile.

"It is not every day you can 'spring' somebody from jail. Maybe I should thank you. A new experience for me. I have to go. We shall speak again soon."

With that Maurice left.

Tom washed his brandy glass and left the flat. He went round the building to where the shops were and asked one of the shop owners where the nearest taxi rank was. The man said it was a long way away but, if Tom wanted, he would telephone a taxi for him. Tom thanked him and said 'yes'.

The taxi came, Tom thanked the shopkeeper and told the taxi driver to take him to Kings Cross station. When Tom got to the station he bought a ticket to Grantham. When Tom arrived at Grantham he got a taxi to his house.

Jenny came out to meet him and gave him a hug. Tom told her everything that had happened while they drank coffee. Jenny listened quietly and when Tom had finished she said, "Things here have been interesting."

Tom was curious.

"Tell me. What has been interesting?"

"I was going to tell you, but you were taken away before I got the chance. I am pregnant."

Tom was shocked but also delighted. He knew that Jenny did not really want more children, she had already had four, but she knew he wanted to have children. He said, smiling from ear to ear, "That's great. Thank you".

Jenny was due to deliver in seven months, but three months after Tom's release he was summoned to court again. Jessica was getting greedy and had applied to have her alimony increased. Tom went to see a solicitor who appointed a barrister on legal aid to speak for Tom. The barrister and Tom met, discussed the situation and the barrister said he would meet Tom at court in two weeks, the date set by the court.

On the day, Tom took the early train to London and went to the County court. His barrister was already there. An hour later Tom and his barrister were called in to court. Jessica was seated with her barrister on the next table at Tom's side.

After the formalities of stating names Jessica's barrister stood up to present his case. He told the judge how hard it was for Jessica to survive on the money that Tom paid. He said that Jessica was not working as she was an actress and she was constantly going to auditions. She could not take another job because she had a bad back.

When he had finished, Tom's barrister stood up to speak. The judge waved him to sit down.

"I have heard enough," the judge said.

He then looked at Jessica.

"I do not believe that a bad back should stop you from taking another job. I am also under the impression that acting can be quite strenuous so the excuse of a bad back does not hold water. If it was in my power, I would award you nothing but the law does not permit this. So, my ruling is that Mr. Levy has to pay his ex-wife six pence a year. That is my ruling. Case dismissed."

They all left court and when outside, Tom saw Jessica's mother glaring at him.

"Can I just give her ten shillings and get it over with?" Tom asked his barrister.

The barrister smiled.

"Definitely not. She might get married and then you will pay nothing."

They both smiled, shook hands and Tom thanked him. It was then back to Grantham.

Two days later Tom got a telephone call from a man who said he was from *The Daily Mail*. The man asked if he had any comments on the ruling that he should pay six pence a year. Tom thought this was one of his friends having a laugh, but he did say that he was pleased it was all over.

The next day there was a very small article in *The Daily Mail* with the headline saying 'Actress gets six pence a year alimony'. Jessica had her say about how unfair the justice system was and Tom was quoted as saying 'how pleased he was it was all over.'

Around the corner from the salon was the market place. In the market place was a fish and chip shop called 'Paddy's'. Tom went there when he wasn't busy because he and Paddy played chess when the shop was quite. They were both very competitive, but Tom had the edge and won more often.

In between one of their games, Paddy said, "I am thinking of franchising the business and retiring. I have somebody in mind to take the shop on."

Tom was thinking about his next move, queen or rook, but replied, with little interest, "Who, do I know him?"

Paddy smiled.

"You."

Tom stopped thinking about his next move.

"Why me? I don't know anything about cooking fish or chips, for that matter."

"I can teach you very easily to do the cooking. You have a good way with people, they like you and I think you will be very successful."

This had taken Tom by surprise and he asked Paddy to give him a couple of days to think about it. Paddy won that game as Tom was distracted.

When Tom got home that evening he told Jenny about his conversation with Paddy. They talked for quite some time and Tom told her that it might be good. He couldn't imagine himself being a hairdresser for the rest of his life. Together they thought it was a good idea and Tom said he would speak to Paddy the next day.

When Tom had a break in his appointment book he went round the corner to see Paddy. They discussed how it would work, with Tom spending a week with Paddy who would show him how the shop runs and how to do the cooking. It was arranged that Tom would start in ten days to allow Tom to give one week's notice to Sergio.

Tom spoke to Sergio and told him about Paddy's offer. Sergio was disappointed but pleased Tom was not going to another salon as there was a possibility that Tom's clients would follow him. Sergio, Gianni and the rest of the staff went for a drink after work on Tom's last day.

The following Monday Tom went to Paddy's and started his training in his new profession. Paddy showed him how to cut the fish into regular portions and how to cook the fish, using a timer. Paddy even made a joke saying it is not good publicity to undercook the fish and poison your customers. They went through everything related to running the shop.

There were forty seats on the restaurant side of the shop and two girls worked in the shop as well as served the tables. The more experienced one was Susan, she had been there three years, and Jill, the other girl had only been there six months.

On the Friday after work, the shop closed at eleven at night.

"You are on your own now," said Paddy, "I wish you luck."

Both men shook hands and Paddy left.

Tom had to be at the shop pretty early. He had to meet reps' and be ready for when the girls arrived. The shop opened at eleven in the morning and closed at two in the afternoon. It then reopened at five o clock in the afternoon and finished for the day at eleven pm.

The girls came to work at ten thirty, but Tom had already done one hour of preparation, cutting the fish and making sure that there were enough potatoes 'chipped'. At two in the afternoon the girls would spend thirty minutes cleaning the tables to be ready for the five o clock opening.

Saturday was market day and the queues would be twenty people deep running outside the shop. Tom started early, ready for the onslaught. It all went fine and they had taken a lot of money.

Tom's daily pattern for during the week was to take the children to town so that they could go to school, then get into the shop for eight thirty. At four in the afternoon he would take the children home and go straight back to work where he would stay until around midnight. It was a long day but the financial rewards were good. Somebody pointed out the apparent riches that Tom had and Tom replied that he did two days' work in one day. He worked sixteen hours a day as opposed to a normal eight hour day.

Tom increased the portion size of the fish. He motivated and trained the staff and business increased. So much so that he took on another member of staff. Susan said she had a friend who was looking for work and Tom told her to bring her friend in for a chat. Susan and her friend arrived the next day a little earlier than usual.

"This is my friend, Wendy," said Susan.

Tom said hello to her and they had a ten minute talk. Tom told her she could start the next day after telling her about the hours and the pay. Wendy was happy with all of this and told Tom she would see him in the morning.

Meanwhile at home, Jenny was getting huge. Their friend, the doctor, said the baby would be coming any day now. Jessy was experienced at having children so she was not too worried, she just wanted 'this lump' to go away. Two days later, a Wednesday, Jenny telephoned Tom.

"Its' coming. Get here now and take me to the hospital."

Tom left Susan in charge and went straight home. He collected Jenny, together with the bag she had packed days ago, and took her to the hospital.

Julien, their son was born the following day. There was one minor accident. While Tom was trying to comfort Jenny, holding her hand and mopping her brow, on one painful contraction, she bit his finger so hard she drew blood. Later, when Jenny was cuddling their new son, Jenny saw Tom's finger bleeding.

"Did I do that?" she asked him, with a little smile.

"Yes," replied Tom.

 "Good, now you know the suffering of childbirth."

They both smiled.

After a year Tom was earning good money. He bought himself a nice car and everything was going well. That was until Paddy came to visit him. Paddy sat at one of the tables and Tom joined him.

"How are things going?" asked Paddy.

"Fine, its' hard work but rewarding."

Paddy had a serious face.

"You know my wife Margaret never wanted for me to retire. She wants me to take the shop back."

Tom was in shock, he thought of Paddy as a friend and they had only a verbal agreement.

"So, what are your plans?" he asked.

"I will give you three more weeks and then you will have to go. Sorry, Tom."

There was nothing Tom could do. He stood up and said, "Ok" and then he went back to work.

Chapter 10

Tom had three weeks in between the hectic hours he worked to find another job! Because of the demands of the shop there was not enough time to look for work and the three weeks disappeared. He had not saved money while working the fish and chips shop. Jenny had bought an array of animals including three goats and the children had been spoilt so Tom needed money coming in immediately.

There was an all-night petrol station on the A1 motorway and Tom went there. He asked to speak to somebody in charge. A man came from the kitchen and asked what he wanted.

"I am looking for work. Do you need anybody?"

"Can you cook? It is only breakfasts," the man said.

"Yes."

"My name is Charlie," the man said, "what is yours?"

"Tom."

"I am looking for a chef for the night job. It is to start at ten at night and work through till eight the next morning. Is that of interest to you?"

Tom thought for a second and firstly it will be some money coming in and secondly, he would have time to look for another job.

"Yes."

Charlie told him the hourly pay, which was less that Tom paid the man to cut his grass, and they agreed that Tom will start that night.

That night Charlie showed Tom where everything was and taught Tom how to make the perfect omelet. At ten o' clock Charlie left Tom to it. The restaurant was very quiet after ten and did not start to get busy until seven thirty the next day. Tom did this during the night and looked for what he called real work during the day.

After three days of this Tom thought that he would have to go back to something he knew he could do and make some money. Hairdressing. He was not going back to Mario's, but he thought he would see if Gerard's would be interested in employing him. In those three days of working in the restaurant, Tom sold his nice car and bought a very old one.

He walked into the reception of Gerard's and a man approached him. The man looked at Tom and said, "I think I know you, are you Tom from Mario's?"

"Yes, I am, and I am looking for a job. Do you have any vacancies?"

The man smiled.

"My name is Gerard. Let's have a talk. Come to the staff room where we won't be disturbed."

Tom and Gerard talked for almost an hour, Gerard wanting to know what happened at Paddy's and Tom telling him that Paddy's wife missed putting her hand in the till whenever she wanted money and there was no formal agreement between himself and Paddy. The conversation ended with Gerard offering Tom a job and agreeing a salary, which included a commission for the money that Tom brought into the salon. Tom was to start the following Monday.

On the Monday, Tom arrived at the salon just before nine o' clock and Gerard introduced him to the rest of the staff.

"As well as myself, Christine is a stylist, she has been with me for eighteen months. We also have two juniors, Ellen and Bridget."

Tom said hello to them all and with that, the first client walked into the salon.

Christine, who was in her early twenties, was tall and slim with dark hair. She had that type of face that she looked like she was always smiling. Ellen, Tom found out later, was eighteen. She had blonde hair and was small and petite. Bridget was short and plump but always seemed happy.

Tom's first few weeks there were quiet, but Grantham being a small market town, word quickly spread that Tom was back in a salon and his clients started to come back to him. It wasn't long before Tom was taking more money than Christine and almost as much as Gerard. Work was going well.

Unfortunately Tom's home life was not quite so good. Jenny's only interest were her animals, she now had three goats, some chickens and four ducks. When Jenny was not playing with the animals she was gardening. Their relationship had diminished to the point of them rarely talking.

Over the next six months Tom sought comfort elsewhere and had some relationships with some of his clients. He did try talking to Jenny and said, "I think we need to talk about our relationship."

Jenny replied, "I am taking the goats for a walk, you can join me."

Tom walked away annoyed as he presumed that the goats were more important than their relationship.

After Tom had been in the salon for six months, he and Ellen started to tease each other. There was obviously a mutual attraction, but Tom was now thirty eight and Ellen was nineteen so romance was out of the question, or so he thought at the time.

One day they were both going to the baker's to buy lunch and Ellen grabbed Tom's hand and pulled him round and passionately kissed him. The teasing in the salon stopped but the kissing outside the salon continued.

Tom was confused as to where this was going. Firstly, Ellen was engaged to be married to Mark, who was her own age, and secondly, after Julien was born, Jenny asked Tom to have a vasectomy which he did.

Two months later Ellen married Mark and Tom took Jenny to the wedding. For Tom this felt strange as his feelings towards Ellen had grown.

The week after the wedding Maurice telephoned Tom, they had kept in touch with at least one phone call a week, sometimes more.

"What is your future in the salon you are working?" said Maurice.

Tom hadn't given this much thought.

"I don't know."

"If you lost a hand would this man keep employing you?"

Tom laughed.

"I wouldn't have thought so."

Maurice then said, in a more serious voice, "I would like to semi retire and I could do this more easily if you joined me here."

Tom thought for a moment. He thought about his relationship with Jenny and he also thought that Ellen would have a better chance of a successful marriage.

He replied to Maurice, "How would this work?"

Maurice had already planned this.

"I have a flat prepared for you, I also have a car you could use and you know where your office is."

He said the last sentence laughing.

"Okay, when do you want to do this?"

"Today is Wednesday, let's say Sunday week, ten days time. I will collect you at midday."

Tom said that would be fine and the conversation ended there.

When Tom got home, Jenny was preparing food in the kitchen. Tom told her to stop and sit down, he did this with authority. Jenny sat down. He told her about his conversation with Maurice and said he would be able to come home weekends and, of course, he would still make sure she had enough money. Jenny did not really care, as long as the money came in, and said it is probably for the best.

Tom told Gerard, who was disappointed, and told him that he would finish work on the Saturday. Gerard wished him luck.

On the Sunday he was to depart Tom spoke to all of the children and told them he was going to work away during the week and he would come home weekends. They were fine with this and each one gave him a kiss and a cuddle. Maurice's Rolls Royce was coming up the track towards Tom's house so Tom found Jenny and said he was going now. She pecked him on the cheek and said goodbye.

When Tom was in the car he asked Maurice if they could make a very quick stop so he could say goodbye to somebody. Maurice agreed. They stopped outside the house that Ellen lived in. After ringing the bell Ellen opened the door.

"I wanted to say goodbye and I wish you every happiness."

Ellen looked sad and tears formed in her eyes.

"Goodbye, Tom."

And she closed the door.

Maurice drove off when Tom was in the car.

"We have one more stop before I take you to the flat," Maurice said. "We are going to *Marks and Spencer* to buy you a couple of suits."

Tom was deep in thought but managed to say, "Thank you."

After they had bought two businesslike suits Maurice took Tom to Eastcote and they parked in the main road outside a shop. By the side of the shop there was a door and Maurice used a key to open it. They went upstairs and Maurice showed Tom where everything was. He had already put food in the fridge for Tom. The flat was only a three minute walk to the office and Maurice told Tom he would give him the car keys when he got to the office, he then left.

Tom sat down on a chair in the kitchen and cried like he had never cried before. He could never have imagined how lonely he could have felt until now.

The next morning Tom dressed in one of his new suits and walked to the office. Maurice met him at the door and told Tom to come with him. They walked outside and Maurice pointed to a blue VW Beetle and handed Tom the keys. Tom thanked him and they went back into the office.

Tom spent the morning looking at some paperwork and familiarizing himself with how the office was run. At two in the afternoon, Mrs. Braithwaite, Maurice's secretary, told Tom there was somebody on the phone for him. She put the call through to Tom's desk.

Tom was confused but could only assume it was Jenny, he had given her his contact details. Tom spoke into the phone and said, "Hello."

It was Ellen's voice that replied.

"I am at the tube station, can you pick me up?"

To say Tom was surprised would be an understatement, but he said, "I will be there in three minutes."

Tom got into the car and drove to the station, Ellen was standing outside. She got into the car and gave Tom a kiss.

"What are you doing here?"

"I have left Mark to be with you."

Tom was shocked but not unhappy, but could see the complication this could bring. He took her back to the flat, let her in and said he would be back soon after five o clock. He then went back to the office.

When Tom got back to the flat he could smell food being cooked. He kissed Ellen and said he would go across the road to the small supermarket and buy a bottle of wine. They ate and talked and then talked some more. Tom telling Ellen the problems they would have and also about him having had a vasectomy. Ellen said she didn't care as long as she could be with him. When they had exhausted the conversation they went to bed.

The next morning Tom went to the office and Maurice had a face of thunder, Tom had never seen him looking so angry.

"Come for a walk," He said to Tom.

Maurice went outside and Tom followed.

"I had a phone call from Jenny. You used me and do not come back to the office. You can have the car until Thursday and then I want the keys back."

Tom nodded and Maurice stormed off going back to the office. Tom was shocked but he could see how Maurice had come to this conclusion.

Chapter 11

When he returned to the flat he told Ellen what had happened. He listed the problems that they faced. No home. No work. No money. And, after Thursday, no form of transport. He told her the first thing they would do was to go back to *Marks and Spencer* and return the suits, that would get them about three hundred pounds. When they got to *Marks and Spencer* they went to the returns department and said that they wanted to return the suits, saying that the job they bought them for no longer existed. The lady behind the counter asked if they had been worn and Tom said no. Whilst she was folding the suits a coin dropped out of one of the pockets. She looked at Tom.

"Family superstition, always put a coin in a new suit," Tom said.

The lady smiled and gave them the refund. They then drove back to the flat.

They went into the kitchen and were surprised to see their mutual friend Stewart sitting in a chair.

"How did you get in?" Tom asked him.

"I went round the back and climbed onto the flat roof and your window was open."

"Why are you here, Stewart?" asked Ellen.

"To take you back to Grantham. All hell's broken loose with not only Mark and Jenny, but your father has now gotten involved. I told them I would come to talk you into coming back."

Ellen was angry.

"I am not coming back so you have wasted you time."

Stewart just nodded and had to accept defeat. He knew it would not end here, but he had done his best. The three of them chatted for a while and Stewart left. The day had been exhausting so after eating they went to bed.

The next day Tom said that they were now social outcast and the only person he thought would still talk to them was his uncle Alf. He lived in Tottenham and they decided that they would visit him. They took the tube to Manor house and then the bus to Tottenham. Tom had always been one of the favorites of uncle Alf and he was pleased to see them. Tom told his uncle the story and his uncle was sympathetic.

The journey from Eastcote to Tottenham took almost two hours so they left uncle Alf's at midday to go back to the flat. Walking from the tube station toward the flat Ellen spotted her father's car. Tom stepped in front of Ellen as he could see there might be trouble. Ellen's father angrily pointed his finger at Tom.

"You keep out of this," he said, "this is between me and my daughter."

"I am not coming back," Ellen screamed at her father.

It was at this point that Mark got out of the car. At the same time Jenny looked out of the flat's window and said to Tom, "Come upstairs and you and I should talk. There won't be any trouble."

Tom looked at Ellen who nodded it would be okay. Tom went upstairs leaving Ellen on the pavement.

When Tom reached the top of the stairs he heard Ellen scream. He ran downstairs as fast as he could only to see Ellen's father's car driving off. He went back up the stairs angry.

"You set me up," he said to Jenny. "You knew that was going to happen."

"Sit down," she replied. "Let's talk this through."

"I have been trying to have a conversation with you for months," Tom angrily replied. "Why now?"

Jenny nodded accepting his last statement. She then said.

"We need to be practical and work out what to do next. Do you want to come back? I am sure that Gerard would take you back."

Tom thought for a moment and realized this was sensible, but said, "No. I am not coming back."

They talked like civilized people for twenty minutes when the doorbell of the flat rang. Tom looked out of the window to see who it was and standing outside the front door was a policeman with Ellen standing behind him. Tom went downstairs and opened the door.

The policeman said to Tom, "Does this young lady belong here?"

"Yes," replied Tom.

With that the policemen nodded and left. Ellen rushed into Tom's arms.

Ellen and Jenny said hello to each other and Jenny asked what had happened. Ellen said that while they were bundling her into the car somebody saw and reported it to the police. The police caught up with her father's car and stopped him. Her father tried to explain that this was his daughter and he was taking her home. The policeman told her father that he could not do this and if her father did not want to be arrested he should drive back to Grantham immediately. Her father then got into the car and drove off.

While the three of them were talking Jenny was ironing her jeans. She had had a very heavy period and washed them. They talked like civilized people until the early hours of the morning and the next topic was how Jenny was to get back to Grantham. Tom told her he would give her money for a taxi to Kings Cross and enough for her train fare. She left soon after two in the morning.

This was to be Tom and Ellen's last night in the flat and tomorrow they would face the unknown. Early the next morning Tom heard a noise downstairs and he went to see what it was. Just inside the front door were two suitcases which, obviously, Maurice had left for them. They packed what little they had in one case and then cleaned and tidied the flat. Once that was done they went out of the flat for the last time, leaving the keys on the kitchen table.

The only thing that Tom could think of doing was to go to the unemployment office to try to find work or, at least, to sign on for benefits. They found out the address of the nearest one and went there. It was a bus ride away. Of the three hundred pounds that they got from returning the suits Jenny had taken one hundred pound of it so they had to be careful with their money.

They walked in to the unemployment office and there were at least twenty people sitting there. There was a little ticket machine which gave you a number to signify where you were in the queue. Their ticket number was thirty three. They sat down and waited till thirty three came up on the screen above the counter.

Tom started to cry as, other than being arrested, he could never have seen himself in this situation. After ninety minutes their number came up on the screen. They spoke to a kindly lady and told her their story. She was sympathetic and asked them where they would sleep tonight. Tom said he did not know and the kindly lady wrote something on a piece of paper and handed it to Tom.

"This is the address of the Social Services office and you should go now and register, maybe they can find you accommodation. I have registered you for benefits and you can come every Friday to collect your money."

They thanked her and left.

The Social Service office was within walking distance, the kindly lady had given them directions. When they arrived there only two people were in front of them. After just fifteen minutes they were seated opposite a woman who was not as friendly as the last lady they had seen. Tom told her their story, she listened and nodded to show that she understood. She then made a phone call and when she put the phone down she said, "Fill out this form, both of you, and then go to this address. They have a room for you in their family home."

Whilst they were filling out their forms, Ellen asked if she could have another form as she had made a mistake. She had written her maiden name down and, of course she now had to use Mark's surname. She corrected this and her married name was now Grimes. When they both completed filling out their forms the lady then made another telephone call telling the person on the other end of the phone their names.

"The house is outside Uxbridge so you may need a map to get there. The lady of the house is Mrs. Walker and she is expecting you."

Both Tom and Ellen thanked her and the left. Opposite the Social Services office was a newsagents and they crossed the road and went in. Tom bought a map of the local area and planned the route to the house.

It took them an hour and a half to get there. Ton rang the doorbell and a lady who looked like she was in her fifties opened the door. She smiled and said, "You must be Ellen Grimes and Tom Levy. Welcome."

They both said in unison, "Thank you."

The landlady opened the door for them both to enter.

"My name is Mrs. Walker. Let me show you round the house and then I will show you your room."

Once again, in unison they both said 'thank you'.

The house can only be described as a typical three bed, semi. As they entered there was a lounge to their left then further into the house was a large kitchen and open plan dining room which looked out to a small garden.

Mrs. Walker opened the refrigerator.

"I have emptied this shelf for you to put any food you want to. Now, let's go upstairs and I will show you your room. There is only me and my husband, the children have moved out, and my husband works nights, so you won't see much of him."

When they got to the landing there were four doors which turned out to be three bedrooms and a bathroom. Mrs. Walker opened one of the doors and said, "This will be your room. I hope you will be happy here. I'll let you settle in and if you want you can come down and I will make us some tea."

It had been a number of days since they felt they could relax and both Tom and Ellen cuddled each other for a few seconds. They were not really in the mood to have tea with this cheerful lady, but felt obligated, so they unpacked the few things they had and went downstairs.

Mrs. Walker made tea and even laid out some cakes for them. It became obvious that she was lonely and was pleased with the company. Tom told her a little of how they were in this situation, enough to satisfy her curiosity. Tom asked where the nearest shops were to buy some food and she gave him directions, it was a five minute walk. They had their tea and some cake and left to go shopping for food.

Their money from returning the suits was diminishing to include the hundred pounds that they gave Jenny, so shopping was to be frugal. They came to the shop which was a small convenience store, grabbed a basket and went round collecting food. They did not know the situation with cooking so they bought salads, cheese and cold meats. Ellen suggested that they buy a small table cloth to put on the floor if they were going to eat in their room. Tom thought this was a good idea.

It would be nine days until Tom could get his unemployment benefit, his registration was too late to collect it this coming Friday so they were very careful with their spending.

The days leading up to Friday a week were mostly spent lazing around in their room but on two occasions the following week Mrs. Walker invited them to eat with her and they also watched some television on those nights.

On the Friday that they were going to collect their benefits money they decided that they would go into central London to buy a *Hairdressers Journal*, the local shops did not sell them.

When they got into central London they found a shop that sold the *Hairdressers Journal* and they decided to treat themselves buy having a coffee. Whilst drinking their coffee Tom looked at the back pages of the journal which was where the job vacancies were. He marked off the ones he thought might be good.

Tom knew he was old in hairdressing terms so he looked for senior positions. There was an advert for a senior stylist in Kingston and after their coffee they found a telephone box and Tom dialed the number. A lady answered the phone.

"Essanelle, how may I help you?"

"I am enquiring whether the position for a senior stylist is still available."

"Mr. Baker, the area manager, is holding interviews here on Monday. Would you like me to book you in?"

Tom said yes and gave his name. The receptionist gave Tom the address and told him to be at the salon at midday.

They went back to their room and planned the journey to Kingston. The rest of the weekend was spent lazing around, but on the Sunday Mrs. Walker invited them for Sunday lunch. They had lost track of the last time they had had a Sunday lunch and they thanked Mrs. Walker.

Early Monday morning they set off to find the salon. They arrived soon after eleven so they went to a café nearby and had a coffee. At eleven fifty they both walked into the salon. The receptionist, who Tom later discovered, was named Julie, looked up when they entered.

"How may I help you?"

Tom said he had come for an interview with Mr. Baker.

"It was me you spoke to last Friday," Julie replied. "Have a seat and I will tell Mr. Baker you are here."

She went to the rear of the salon and came back within seconds.

"Mr. Baker will see you now. Please follow me."

Tom followed her to the rear of the salon and she opened a door and ushered Tom in.

Mr. Baker was seated behind a desk. He looked to be in his mid thirties, younger then Tom, and he stood up to shake hands.

"Hello. I am Mike Baker, the area manager, and you are Tom?"

Tom shook his hand and said, "Yes. Thank you for seeing me, Mr. Baker."

"Call me Mike. Now tell me a little about yourself."

Tom told him the stories of him working in salons, he did not mention the fish and chips shop. Mike listened intently. When Tom had finished Mike said, "You are not a senior stylist. You need a management job. I can offer you the assistant manager's job in Horsham. Would that interest you?"

"Yes, that would, thank you. By the way, my girlfriend, who is in the reception, is an excellent hairdresser."

Mike's thinking was, I can kill two birds with one stone here if she is any good. Solve the senior stylist position here and the assistant manager's job in Horsham.

They got one of the staff prepared to have her hair done by Ellen. Ellen got on well with her and they chatted a lot. Ellen got the job as a senior stylist. Salaries were agreed and they both were to start work the following Monday.

The next project for them was to find somewhere to live in the Horsham area. The train journey from Kingston to Horsham was just over thirty minutes. When they arrived in Horsham Tom bought a local newspaper to look for accommodation. They took the newspaper to a café, ordered coffee and studied the section of rental properties.

With their benefits money and what they had saved they had a little under three hundred pounds so whatever place they got would have to be cheap. Tom showed Ellen an advert for a one bedroom flat in Billingshurst. Tom told her that they passed Billingshurst two stations before getting to town. It was also good for Ellen because the train went right to Kingston where she would work. The other big benefit was that because it was out of the town it was almost half the price of the rentals in town.

The rent was advertised for eighty pounds a month and one month's rental as a deposit. If they paid this, they would have just under one hundred and forty pounds for the rest of the

month   Mike had told them that the

company paid monthly, for food and travel. It was tight but doable.

They telephoned the person renting the place and arranged to be there within the hour. Two stops on the train and they were in Billingshurst. It was more a village than a town and the flat was opposite a church. Tom knocked on the door and it was opened by an older lady. She introduced herself saying, "Hello, my name is Mrs. Smith. Please come in."

She opened the door wider and they both walked into a large lounge. The bedroom was to the left and the small kitchen was at the back of the property.

Tom and Ellen introduced themselves and they both looked at each other, smiled and nodded that they liked the place. Tom asked Mrs. Smith if they could move in next Saturday and Mrs. Smith agreed. She was aware that the place had been empty and earning no money for the last four months so she was happy.

They all shook hands and arranged to meet at midday next Saturday. For Tom and Ellen this meant, staying at Mrs. Bakers gave them five more days without paying rent.

When they got back to Uxbridge they told Mrs. Baker that they had found work and they would be leaving on Saturday morning. She said she was pleased for them, but would miss them as she had enjoyed their company.

"As a celebration, I shall cook you both a meal tomorrow," Mrs. Baker added.

On the Saturday they said goodbye and thanked Mrs. Baker for her kindness. Tom told Ellen on their way to the station he thought he saw a tear in Mrs. Baker's eye as they said their final goodbyes. After an hour and a half travelling they arrived at Billingshurst station. They were at the flat at eleven thirty and were surprised to find Mrs. Smith already there.

Tom paid Mrs. Smith and she gave them two sets of keys and wished them luck. Tom and Ellen explored what was in the flat. They were pleased to find that there was ample crockery, mugs and cooking utensils. There was also enough bedding and the only thing that they would need to buy was towels and food.

They both went to the local shop and bought a large chicken hoping it would last three days. One day they would have it with roast potatoes, the next they would have it with mash potatoes and the third day they would have it with salad. There was no television in the flat so Tom bought a pack of cards and also a scrabble set. After they had deposited their purchases back to the flat, as it was a nice day they decided to go for a walk. They walked hand in hand and for the first time, in what felt like months, they were happy and the future looked better.

On the Monday morning they both went to the station. Tom bought tickets for both of them and Ellen crossed the bridge so that she was on the opposite side to Tom. Ellen arrived at the salon in Kingston and was introduced to all of the staff. There were five stylists plus her and four juniors. As well as these there was the manager and the receptionist. She was later to discover that Kingston was one of the 'flagships' of Essanelle.

Tom got off of the train, it was only a four minute walk to the salon which was in the centre of town. He walked into the reception area and there was a young lady sitting at the desk. She looked up and smiled.

"You must be Tom. I was told to expect you. Please, have a seat. My name is Glenda and I am the manageress here."

Tom sat down and said, "Hello. It is nice to meet you too."

Glenda, who was still smiling then said, "Mike, the area manager told me you were coming as my assistant manager. I am sure we will do well together. As the rest of the staff come in, we are early, I shall introduce you and then show you round the salon."

Tom thanked her. She looked in her early thirty's and was not what you would call slim and she had blonde hair, not naturally.

The first to walk through the door was a young man, maybe mid twenties.

"This is Gareth, our senior stylist," Glenda said. "Gareth, this is Tom and he is here as my assistant."

Tom stood up and shook Gareth's hand. Gareth then left. The next two to walk in together were Susan and Rita, they were both juniors. Glenda introduced them all the same as she had with Gareth. Another young man walked in, maybe early twenties, thought

Tom. Introductions were made as before. Finally, a young lady walked in, about the same age as Paul, and Tom had met the whole staff.

Glenda told Tom to have a walk round the salon to familiarise himself. The first thing that Tom noticed while he was in the reception was the prices, almost double what he charged in Grantham. In the salon there were six works station and four backwashes. There was also a row of three hair dryers. The salon furniture was not only modern, it was of a good quality.

Tom spent most of the day just watching the staff work. Soon after midday Glenda told Tom that she had set up a column for him to take appointments. Tom thanked her. The next few days went in a similar pattern, but it became obvious to Tom that the staff did not think much of Glenda. He overheard them saying derogatory remarks and saying she was lazy.

Every evening when Ellen got home they would spend the first hour telling each other how their day was. It would be true to say that this was the happiest they had both been for a very long time. The first month flew by and then there was something to really celebrate, two pay packets. Ellen was sad how things had worked out with her father and whenever she thought about this she felt guilty. Tom encouraged her to get in touch and try to speak to him.

"The worst that can happen is he won't speak to you. At least you would have tried."

Ellen plucked up the courage one lunchtime. She went to a telephone booth and dialed her father's number. He was so pleased to hear from her and they arranged that Ellen would go and see him and her mother that weekend. Ellen came home that night very happy and told Tom about the conversation and the arrangement to go and visit them this coming weekend. She asked Tom if he minded.

"Not at all," he said, "I am really pleased for you."

With that he gave her a hug and a kiss.

Ellen left for Ipswich, this is where her parents lived, early Saturday morning. With the changes in trains the journey took almost three hours. When she got to Ipswich station she telephoned her father and he came to the station to collect her. He got out of the car when he saw her and gave her a hug. There were tears of pleasure running down his cheeks. As soon as Ellen got in the car she started to tell the 'story', but her father said, "Not now, your mother will want to hear it."

The rest of the five minute journey was in silence.

When they got home Ellen's mother came out to the street and nearly suffocated Ellen with her hug. When they got into the bungalow that her parents lived in Ellen told them the full story. With the coffee breaks this took almost three hours. When she had finished her father said, "Where is he?"

"Firstly he did not know what sort of reception he would get, and secondly, he thought it better that we all talk first," Ellen replied.

"Next time you come I want you to bring him."

The afternoon and evening passed quickly as Ellen remembered things that she had missed out when tell her parents the story the first time. There were three happy people in that house. Ellen eventually went to bed in the spare room and fell asleep quickly.

On the Sunday morning they all had breakfast together as Ellen was going to catch the lunchtime train back to Billingshurst and dreaded the three hour journey. When Ellen eventually got back to the flat she told Tom how well it had gone. He said how pleased he was for her because he could see how happy she was. She also told Tom that her farther wanted him to go with her the next time she goes.

Chapter 12

After Tom had been at the Horsham salon for three months Mike Baker came to the salon. He normally came every two weeks but this time he wanted to speak to Tom.

"How are you enjoying it here?" said Mike when Tom was in the office and seated.

"It is good and will be better when I get busier," Tom replied, smiling.

Mike looked serious.

"Tom, I am going to move Glenda to another salon and I want you to take over as manager here. How does that sound?"

"That would be great. Thank you."

"This salon is budgeted to take eighteen hundred a week, it is doing twelve hundred. Can you get it better?"

"I can promise you, I will do everything I can to make it better."

Within two weeks Glenda was gone. At the end of the day Tom called a full staff meeting.

"You lot are my problem now," said Tom with a smile when everybody was gathered round.

The staff smiled back.

"Do we want to be losers, the worst salon in the group? I don't think so and I am sure that you all want a good career. Let's start with something simple. Our retail should be five percent. It is one percent. I am going to put a pound into a box and I want you all to do the same. We will make a competition and whoever does the most retail sales takes the money. What do you all think?"

They all thought that this sounded fun and there were a couple of them saying, 'Yeah, great idea.'

Tom said a few more things about having fun and letting the clients enjoy being with us. He finished by saying. "Let's show this bloody Head Office how good we are."

The rest of the staff cheered, smiled and went home. Tom had always been good at motivating people, even in his school football team he had been made captain.

The retail paper was stuck on the wall and every time a sale was made there was a tick against that person's name. There was more laughter and more fun throughout the salon, staff nicely teasing each other, clients getting involved and they all got busier earning more in commission.

In three months the salon was up to budget, eighteen hundred pounds a week. Mike Baker came more often to not only pat Tom on the shoulder, but to praise the rest of the staff. Within the next three months the salon was taking more than two thousand two hundred pounds a week. The staff, through their commission, had increased their salary by fifty percent. Tom even gave a raise to the juniors because they were not on commission.

In the meanwhile, Ellen was doing well and had built up a good clientele. Daren, her manager was constantly telling her how pleased he was of her. One day he called her into his office and told her to sit down.

"I am leaving," he said when she was seated. "I have been offered the manager's job across the road at Glemby."

Ellen was a bit shocked, but wondered why he was telling her and not the rest of the staff.

"I am pleased for you. Well done," she said, smiling.

"You are probably wondering why I am telling you."

"Yes, I am."

"I want you to come with me. What do you think? I will be able to pay you more money."

Ellen was in a state of shock but managed to say, "That sounds great. Let me know when."

Essanelle and Glemby were both American companies and they were both worldwide with salons in many countries. Glemby was the larger of the two with over seventeen hundred salons worldwide. Darren left two weeks later and arranged for Ellen to join him two weeks after that.

Two days after Darren left Mike Baker came to the Horsham salon. He told Tom he wanted a private word with him and they went into Tom's office.

"Tom, you have done a good job here," Mike said when they were seated, "but I think you are ready for a new challenge. I want to move you to our flagship salon in Kingston. What are your thoughts on this?"

It is true that now Tom had got things working as he wanted he was getting bored.

"That would be great, would there be more money?"

He smiled a cheeky smile when he asked that question.

"I think we can arrange this," said Mike, smiling.

Mike and Tom chatted about how the transition would work. Tom said that Gareth would make a great manager and he could employ and junior stylist, at half the salary that Tom got, and he thought that would work. The move was arranged for two weeks time. This worked out well as Ellen would leave the salon as Tom joined it.

The weekend before they were due to start their new jobs Ellen had arranged to visit her parents. Her father insisted she bring Tom with her. They both set off on the Saturday morning for the three hour journey. When they eventually got to Ipswich Ellen's father was waiting in the car park. Ellen noticed he had changed his car. It was now a yellow Fiat. Ellen gave her father a hug and Tom and her father shook hands without saying anything.

Tom went to sit in the back and Ellen went to the passenger side of the car.

"Stop," Ellen's father said.

She looked at him and he was holding the car keys toward her. She thought he wanted her to drive so she shrugged and went round to the driver's side and got in. Her father got in the passenger side of the car.

"Did you not want to drive, dad?" Ellen said to her father.

He smiled.

"I don't like driving somebody else's car. This is yours."

Tears of guilt flowed down Ellen's cheek, she felt so guilty for treating them so bad.

"Thank you, dad," she managed to mumble. "I don't know what to say."

He laughed.

"Say nothing then. Just drive us home."

When they got back to the house the atmosphere was a little tense between Ellen's mum and Tom, but it eased as time went by. By the evening they were all friends with Ellen's father telling Tom to look after his girl.

Ellen's mother had made an evening meal for all of them and, under the circumstance, the evening was quite pleasant. On the Sunday morning Ellen and Tom set off for their drive to the flat, the journey only took just under two hours.

The next day, Monday, they set off to Kingston in the car. The journey took forty five minutes because when they got near Kingston the traffic was bad. Ellen found a place to park, not easy in Kingston, without having to pay, and they both went to their new jobs.

Tom walked into the salon and Julie was sitting at her desk. She said.

"Good morning," she said. "Do you want me to introduce you to the rest of the staff?"

"No, thanks, I will get to talk to them as the day progresses."

Tom knew where his office was, it was where Mike had originally interviewed him. He went in and sat down and pulled out some papers which showed him how the salon was doing. He also noticed, while he was at the reception, the prices here were fifty percent higher than Horsham. The salon, according to his budgets was meant to be taking just over three thousand pounds a week but was only averaging two thousand three hundred.

He spent the morning looking through the papers and telephoned the reception. Julie answered.

"Yes, boss?"

"As the staff become free, can you send them into my office please. I think I prefer to meet them this way."

"Okay," Julie said.

Ten minutes later there was a knock on Tom's door.

"Come in," Tom yelled.

A young man entered. He was about eighteen and wore the uniform of a junior. Tom told him to sit down and asked his name.

"I am Dave and I have been here for two years," The young man said.

Tom had a piece of paper in front of him so he could make a note of who was who. He wrote down Dave's name and asked him a few questions, how do you like it here, what do you want to do when you finish your apprenticeship and a few questions about his private life. This finished in fifteen minutes and he thanked Dave and told him to go back to work.

At the end of the day Tom had spoken to everyone and his list read: Ricky. Senior stylist. Preferred men to women. Robert. Stylist. Been with the company for eighteen months. Linda. Stylist. Been with the company for one year. Theresa (preferred to be called Terry) Junior stylist. Been with the company for six months. Susan (Preferred to be called Sue). Junior. She had been with the company for one year. And, finally. Greta. Junior. Been with the company for six months.

Tom spent the next few weeks mainly in the salon. He was going round and talking to the clients and having fun with the staff. Their reaction to him was good and they responded well to his advice. Different ways to treat their clients. He even gave training to the juniors and made them feel part of the team.

Julie said to him that it was more fun than before he came. All of the stylists, if they were not busy, did the same as Tom and went and spoke to the clients of other stylists. They were all becoming a team. After six weeks this was reflected in the takings. They were now only a couple of hundred pounds short of the projected budget. This means that they had average five hundred pounds a week better than before Tom came.

The next year went really well. Ellen was making more money with the raise in her basic salary and lots of her clients from Essanelle had heard where she was and had come back to her so her commission was also good. Tom had gotten two more rises because of what he had done with the salon.

The car was much less expensive than their train fares and they had started to save some money.

On a Friday evening Ellen told Tom that Darren, her manager, had said his area manager had wanted to speak to Tom. Tom asked her what it was about but she didn't know. Tom said to her to arrange this. On the following Monday on their way home Ellen told Tom she arranged a meeting with Darren's area manager for midday the next day. Tom said that would be fine.

The following day at midday Tom walked across the road to the store that Glemby's salon was in. He went to the reception and told the receptionist that he had an appointment with Mr. Mackay. She told him to take a seat. She picked up the phone and spoke quietly into it. Thirty seconds later a man approached Tom. Tom stood up and the man held out his hand to be shook. Tom shook his hand.

The man smiled and said, "Hello, Tom. Thank you for coming. My name is George Mackay and I am the divisional manager for Glemby. Please come into my office."

He put his hand on Tom's shoulder to lead him towards his office. When they arrived at a door George opened it and went in. Tom followed him in and he sat in the chair opposite him.

George smiled at Tom.

"We have been watching your career with Essanelle, you have done well."

"Thank you," Tom said.

"We would like to offer you an area manager's job in East Anglia."

The package that George offered Tom was good. The salary would be three thousand pounds a year more than Tom was earning now. There was also a company car on offer. Tom was told that he would be based in Cambridge. Tom asked George if he could have two days to think about it and George agreed. Tom told him he would telephone him.

On their way home Tom told Ellen about his conversation with George. She was really excited. As well as the extra money they would be one step closer the where she wanted to live, Ipswich, where her parents lived.

Two days later Tom telephoned George to accept his offer but pointed out that Ellen would still need to work. George told him that he would be based in Cambridge and Ellen could work in that salon. That weekend they drove to Cambridge to look for properties. They had enough money for a deposit for something not too expensive. They saw a flat for sale in a village just outside Cambridge named Hardwick. It was a one bedroomed flat and was on sale at thirty four thousand pounds. With a deposit of five percent they could afford this.

After seeing the flat they drove back to the agents and put in an offer for the full price. There next visit was to a Building Society to arrange a mortgage. This proved successful and the wheels were in motion for them to buy their first property together. On the following Monday Tom used the telephone book to contact a solicitor in Cambridge. He gave the solicitor all of the information and the solicitor told him he will deal with it.

In spite of the fact that Tom telephoned the solicitor every day there was no way the sale would be completed by the time they both had to move to Cambridge so Ellen arranged with her parents that they could stay at their house. It was only one hour drive away.

Much to Mike's disappointment, he accepted Tom's resignation. They collected their things from Hardwick and drove to Ipswich over the weekend and moved into Ellen's parents' bungalow.

On the Monday morning both Ellen and Tom took their cars to Cambridge. Tom told her he wanted to check in at the salon in Cambridge and then drive over to Norwich. Tom left at seven thirty so he could do the things he wanted. Ellen left the house at eight, this would give her time to get to the salon and find a parking place, not an easy task in Cambridge.

The salon in Cambridge was in a store called Eden and Lilly. It was on the third floor. Tom parked in the underground car park and took the lift to the third flood. When the doors of the lift opened he saw the salon opposite. He walked in to the salon and sitting at the reception desk was a lady, possibly in her forties. She was quite plump, but had a lovely smile when Tom walked in.

"Are you Tom, the new area manager?"

"Yes. And you are?"

"I am Pat, the manageress and also the manicurist. It is nice to meet you. I was told there would be two of you coming, is that true?"

"My friend, Ellen, will be here soon, but I wanted some time with you first. Tell me about the salon, Pat."

Pat told him she had been at the salon for five years. There was another stylist named Sandra who had been there for four years and a junior named Theresa, she liked to be called

'Terry', who had been at the salon for six months. She added, we had another stylist, her name was Brenda, but she has just left she then added that she hoped that Ellen would take her place. She also said the store had been in existence for over a hundred years and, Pat joked, most of the customers were children when it opened.

Tom smiled.

"Are you happy here, Pat?"

"Yes, but there is little excitement," she replied.

Soon after this some of the staff came in and, just before nine o' clock, Ellen entered. Pat went straight to Ellen and took her to the staff room for a chat.

Tom, after saying hello to the girls that came in, looked at the figures that the salon produced. He spent an hour on this and then told Pat that he was leaving. He said he was going to Norwich and should be there in an hour if anybody wanted him.

Tom went to his company car, it was a brand new Ford, and he drove to Norwich. The Norwich salon was small with just three staff and Tom spent some time talking to the manageress. After two hours Tom realized that if he left now he would have time to visit the salon in Ipswich.

The salon in Ipswich was based in one of the peripheral shops at the entrance of a supermarket. There was only three staff there but the manageress told him that there were two more but, because the opening hours were long, they had a shift system. It was after seven before he left there and went to Ellen's parents' house.

Chapter 13

The days for Tom and Ellen followed a similar pattern. Ellen had settled in well and got on well with Pat. She found it easier to get new clients because the 'footfall' was quite large.

Tom had nine salons to oversee. They were in Norwich, Colchester, Ipswich, Watford, Tottenham, Bury St Edmunds, Chelmsford and of course Cambridge. His day started early, depending on the journey, normally soon after six o clock, and finished late, normally after seven. The time spent with the managers was educational and motivational and he befriended them all.

After two months he even had the managers telephoning him on a Saturday night to say how well their week was. It was after this two month period he heard from his solicitor that the sale of the flat was ready to complete so he made Cambridge his next salon to visit. Pat allowed Ellen time off to go with Tom to sign the final papers. They could move into the flat the next day. It was theirs!

They had no furniture, cooking equipment, bed sheets or anything else. The flat was bare. Some of the furniture they bought was second

hand, but the cooker and fridge were new.
Also new were the bedsheets and towels.
Ellen's parents helped with the buying of the
fridge and the cooker.

It was a week after the completion of the sale
of the flat that they were ready to move in.
Ellen took most of the responsibility of
accepting the deliveries because Tom was on
the road most of the time. They moved in to
their first bought property on the weekend.

Over the next six months, Ellen was happy
and had now obtained a good size clientele.
Tom had got his area to increase sales by
almost twenty percent but the 'bottom line'
(the percentage of profit) had increased to
fourteen percent.

On one of Tom's visits to Head Office he met
Clive, they had met many times before as
Clive was Tom's immediate superior. Clive
was a Divisional Vice President for the
South. Ray was the Divisional Vice President

for the north. Tom had notice recently that Clive was becoming quite cold towards him.

When the managing director, Tony Allbright, went to the toilet Tom followed. Whilst they were standing Tom said to Tony, "Clive seems to be a little cold towards me, is there a reason?"

Tony laughed.

"Maybe a little better if we talk in my office."

Once hands were washed Tom followed Tony to his office. Tony gestured for Tom to sit.

"Have I created a problem?" Tom asked.

Tony laughed.

"No, Tom, you are doing a great job and we are pleased with you. The situation you have with Clive." And here he hesitated for the right words. "Tom. You are not the most humblest of men. I, and everybody else, is aware of what you have achieved, but some might call you arrogant. You do not mix with the other area managers or any staff. People here are used to 'sucking up' to senior managers. You don't, and that makes people suspicious."

Tom thought about this. He believed that his success was enough and he wasn't used to politics.

"What should I do?"

"Exactly what you are doing, but your success is making others feel uncomfortable. Just carry on, but try to be more friendly."

Two weeks after the meeting in the toilet Tony invited Tom to join him. He was taking the owner of a store in Colchester to a restaurant for lunch, tomorrow. Tony told Tom he would pick him up in Cambridge and they could travel in one car, Tony's.

On the next day Tom was in the salon in Cambridge and, at eleven, Tony arrived. Tony had a few words with Pat, the manageress and together with Tom, they went to where Tony had parked his car.

The journey started off in silence but when Tony was on the main road he said to Tom, "So, tell me how you are doing. I know the numbers from your stores so I want to know how you, personally are doing."

Tom thought for a moment.

"Do you want me to be totally honest?"

"I would prefer it."

Tom was thinking how to word this. Eventually he said, "When I first started I was doing a fourteen hour day. I loved it and the managers responded well. Now, other than to brag how well they are doing, they don't really need me. I could easily start at ten and finish at four and, you asked for honesty, I am bored."

Tom breathed a sigh of relief that he had got that out. Tony just smiled. After a minute's silence Tony said, "I am aware that you want more and you will have. Clive and myself are working on something, something quite exciting for you, and we shall probably ask

you to come to Head Office next week."
Tony then smiled and said to Tom teasingly,
"Do you think you can wait that long?"

Tom said yes and the rest of the drive was in
silence with both men lost in their own
thoughts.

On Mondays, Tom was always at the
Cambridge salon. He would collect the
figures from the other managers and do
whatever paperwork needed doing. At eleven
o' clock Tom was called to the phone at the
reception. He picked it up and it was Tony's
secretary asking him to come to Head Office
at midday tomorrow. Tom said he would. He
replaced the handset and, with a sense of
anticipation, started to get excited.

The next morning Tom drove to central
London. He parked his car and arrived at
Head Office just before midday. He sat in the
reception area waiting to be called. After a

few minutes Tony's secretary told Tom to go to Tony's office.

Tom knocked lightly on the door and entered. Tony was sitting behind his desk and facing him in one of the chairs was Clive.

"Take a seat," Tony said to Tom.

All three of them said hello. Tony was first to speak.

"After our conversation last week I have been talking to Clive."

Clive smiled and nodded.

Tony continued.

"You know of the Stewart's Group of stores and you know that for us they are big business. Combined, they bring in just over twenty five percent of our total business here in the UK."

Tony paused to make sure that Tom was with him and then continued.

"They are not happy with our performance and they are talking about using another company for their concession. This would be a disaster for us. The divisional manager in charge of that group has left. We agreed with him it was by mutual consent. Clive and myself think that you could pull it round."

Tony again paused.

"Tom, it would mean a promotion and you would become a divisional manager with a salary that was commensurate with that position. It would also mean an upgrade car for you. How does that sound to you?"

Tom was stunned. He wanted more work but this was something he could never imagined. He smiled and said to Tony, "That will be great. Thank you both for the opportunity."

He was careful not to leave out Clive in his thanks. Clive then spoke.

"Tom, we will start this next week as we need to show the stores that we are taking this seriously. I will get all of the paperwork to you by tomorrow so you can study it together with a list of the stores and the current managers running our salons. Leave the car to me and I will find you something nice."

Clive smiled at the last sentence.

The meeting ended there and Tom left. When Tom got home that night he told Ellen about the meeting with Tony and Clive. Ellen was delighted for him and thought to herself this could be the opportunity for them to move to Ipswich. After all, it did not really matter where they lived as long as Tom could get to his new salons. Tom then said that they should go out for a meal to celebrate.

Tom and Ellen showered and changed and Tom drove to the restaurant. When they were seated and had their drinks served Ellen, knowing that Tom was in a good mood, decided to talk about a move to Ipswich. She smiled at Tom and said, "We have been in our flat for just over seven months and I know that prices have risen. If we could make a profit of ten thousand pounds and add this to the small deposit we put down plus your raise in salary, do you think we could afford a deposit for a house in Ipswich?"

Tom smiled and knew that was her hearts' desire. He said. "For the next three to six months I am going to be very busy. If you want to do the research, find out how much we can sell the flat for, get an idea of the prices of houses in Ipswich and speak to a Building Society about a mortgage, I am happy to look to a move."

Ellen thought this might be one of the happiest days of her life. She reached across and squeezed Tom's hand and blew a kiss across the table.

The next day Tom again went to Cambridge which is where his office was. Soon after ten o' clock Tom received a fax which was several pages long from Clive. He sat down to study them.

There were only five salons, but all of them were budgeted to take a lot of money. The one that stood out was in Croydon, it had a budget of taking two and a half million pounds a year. Currently it was taking one point eight million pounds a year. Tom read that Malcolm, who managed the Bromley salon very successfully, had been promoted to the Croydon salon. The result of this was that the Bromley salon's taking had gone down and the slide in the Croydon salon had continued. Tom decided that Croydon was the first salon he would visit.

The other three salons did not represent such a major problem as their takings against budget, although not good, did not make so much difference to the five million that the group should be aiming for.

Tom spent the next couple of hours going through the P&Ls (profit and loss) of all of the salons. He decided there was room for improvement on both fronts, the income and the expenses. He then planned his strategy. The following Monday would be spent all day in Croydon speaking to Malcolm and some of the staff. On the Tuesday he would go to Bromley and speak to the staff there.

The next three days Tom visited all of his nine salons to keep his managers enthused. He told them all that they were doing such a great job that he would be seeing them less but they should keep him informed as to how well they were doing.

Over the weekend Ellen told Tom that she had looked at prices of similar flats to theirs and the average price was selling for forty seven thousand, thirteen thousand pounds more than they paid for theirs. If they could make an extra thirteen thousand plus the fifteen hundred they put down as a deposit that should be enough for a deposit on a house in Ipswich. Tom smiled at her excitement and told her to carry on working on this project.

On the Friday Tom telephoned Malcolm to tell him that he would meet him at the salon early Monday morning. He asked Malcolm if he would mind doing the weekly paperwork over the weekend so they could both have some time together. All managers had to have the weekly paperwork done by midday to be faxed off to Head Office. Malcolm said that would be no problem and the conversation ended there.

On Monday morning Tom was up early. He knew the journey to Croydon would take at least one and a half hours and he wanted to be at the salon by eight thirty. He left home at six thirty to make sure he was on time. He arrived at Croydon town centre soon after eight but it took him twenty minutes to get his car parked.

The Stewart's store was very large and four stories high. When Tom entered he had to go through the perfumery department and he then saw a sign showing which floor every department was. The salon was on the third floor. He went up the escalators to the third floor and saw the entrance to the salon in the corner of this space.

Tom walked into the salon and sitting behind a desk in the reception area was a pretty young lady. Tom noticed she had a badge which said, "Lisa. HeadReceptionist.'

She looked at Tom, smiled and said, "How may I help you?"

"I am Tom Levy and am here to meet Malcolm."

Lisa was pre-warned that Tom was coming and told who he was. She smiled and told Tom to take a seat and she would let Malcolm know he was here. She picked up the phone and spoke into it.

Thirty seconds later a man, probably in his mid thirties, came into the reception. He walked straight up to Tom. Tom stood and they both shook hands. Malcolm was first to speak.

"Hello, I am Malcolm. Pleased to meet you."

"Hello, Malcolm. Good to meet you too."

"Why don't we go into my office, we will have more privacy there?"

"Good idea," Tom said.

Malcolm walked into the salon. It was huge with at least twenty work stations and rows of backwashes as well as rows of drying banks. They walked to the back of the salon and Malcolm opened a door and entered his office. His office was the size of a small salon with a desk in the centre and filing cabinets around the walls. Malcolm sat behind his desk and Tom took the seat opposite him.

"Would you like a coffee or tea?" Malcolm asked when they were both seated

"No, thanks."

Tom then started the conversation asking Malcolm if he was enjoying it here and Malcolm replied, with a little hesitation, he was. They went through some figures together and Tom, through the conversation, discovered that Malcolm was married, had two children and had been moved from Bromley to Croydon seven months ago.

After two hours, Tom said he would like to speak to the assistant manager if she was free. Tom had studied the senior structure of the salon and knew her name was Adriana. Malcolm said he would check if she was free and send he into the office. When he had left, Tom continued to look through the accounts.

A minute later a young lady, probably about twenty five years old, knocked and entered the office. She was petite and had dark hair and a nice smile.

"Hello," she said, "my name is Adriana, I am the assistant manager."

With that, she took a seat opposite Tom. Tom smiled.

"I imagine you know who I am. It is nice to meet you, Adriana."

Tom asked Adriana how long she had been in the salon, she replied, nine months. He asked her where she had worked before and a little about her personal life, married, children etc.

"How do you and Malcolm get on?"

Adriana hesitated a little and said, "We get on well. Malcolm is a nice guy. Maybe too nice."

Tom's curiosity peaked.

"What do you mean by, too nice?"

Adriana decided that this was a man that wanted the truth and just told honestly so she said, "When you have a salon with sixteen stylists, most of them prima donnas, they do not want a friend, they need, a manager. Somebody who they will respect."

"Are you saying that Malcolm is not respected?"

Adriana hesitated.

"As I mentioned before, Malcolm is a nice guy but, if you are asking me to be totally honest, no."

Tom spoke a little more to Adriana and she was called into the salon as her client had arrived. Malcolm came back into the office and asked Tom how it was going. Tom decided that he needed some time to think and told Malcolm that he was going to the restaurant in the store for a sandwich and a coffee and he will be back in half an hour.

Tom found the restaurant on the floor above. He ordered coffee and a chicken sandwich and found a vacant table. It was now 'thinking time'. Tom didn't think that Malcolm was comfortable here, his hesitation in his reply to Tom asking. Adriana was ambitious and came across as very strong. After Tom had finished eating and drinking he went back to the salon. Malcolm saw him and gestured for both of them to go back to the office.

Tom was first to speak.

"Malcolm, I have a problem which you may be able to solve. This group of salons spends almost a quarter of a million pounds a year on stock. It is time consuming for me to go through it every month and I need some help. Would you be interested in helping me out?"

Malcolm felt very privileged to have been asked. He smiled and said, "I would be delighted to."

"The problem we have is that looking after the stock is time consuming and running this salon would be too much. How would you feel about going back to Bromley?"

If he were to be honest with himself, he was delighted. Bromley was so much easier to run and he hadn't been happy here. Also, Tom would give him the job of looking after a quarter of a million pounds' worth of stock. An honour indeed.

"I would be happy to go back and be able to help you with the stock. Thank you for the opportunity," he said.

Tom asked Malcolm to ask Adriana to come back into the office when she was free to do so. Malcolm said he would. Tom sat by himself and looked again at the figures.

Twenty minutes later Adriana came back into the office and took the seat opposite Tom. Tom asked her how she would feel about managing this salon.

"I would love that. I already have in mind some of the things I would change and some of the staff. I want to build a strong team and not a bunch of individuals that we have at the moment."

Tom was pleased with this response and then asked her if she was competent with the paperwork.

"I do most of it already," she replied smiling.

Tom discussed the salary and a lot of it was on performance. Adriana was happy with this as she was sure she would be successful.

Two hours later Tom said goodbye to Malcolm, Adriana and any other member of staff that he walked past. When he was in his car and driving home he thought that this was a good day's work.

Over the rest of the week Tom went to the Bromley salon, they were delighted that Malcolm was coming back, he also went to the Tonbridge, Basildon and Seven Oaks salons and spoke to all the managers there.

Over the next three months Tom spent every day going to one salon or another, sometimes two salons a day if the visits were short. He concentrated on the Croydon salon and how Adriana was getting on. She was friendly but firm with the staff and was made for a management roll.

The figures after three months showed positive signs. Bromley was now back on target and Croydon had already increased by twenty percent. Both Clive and Tony had telephoned him a few times to say that they were happy with how things were going and the Stewart group was also pleased.

The reason that the Stewart group was pleased was because they get a percentage of the salons takings and this had increased.

In the meantime Ellen had done her 'homework' regarding buying a house in Ipswich. Their flat had gained twelve thousand pounds since they had bought it and, together with the small deposit they had put to buy the flat, was enough of a deposit to buy a house. Also, Tom was now earning pretty good money.

Ellen found a house she liked on the Stoke Park Estate, a suburb of Ipswich, and they went to see it. They both fell in love with it and bought it and five weeks later they moved into it.

Tom did his motivational chat to all of the salons and every three months he got all fourteen managers under his control to come to Croydon to have an open meeting. They would talk about the things they had done their salon and give each other advice and encouragement. Malcolm was doing a good job with the stock telling Tom if a salon had exceeded their budget. His stock control was excellent.

After a year, Tom's 'bottom line' (Percentage of profit) was eighteen percent while the company as a whole was twelve percent. Eighteen months after Tom joined Glemby, Tony telephoned Tom and asked him to come to the office.

When Tom arrived at Head Office he was told to go straight to Tony's office. He knocked gently on the door and Tony called out, "Come in."

When Tom entered he saw that there was also Clive and Raymond there. He knew that Raymond was a Divisional Vice President, the same as Clive, for the North of the country.

"Take a seat, Tom," Tony said.

There was only one vacant chair so Tom sat on it.

"Tom, we are pleased with the work you have done and we have a proposition for you."

Tom sat a little further forward on his chair and waited for Tony to continue. Tony did continue.

"How would you like to move to the north. You will have twenty seven salons to manage and be assisted by three area managers and possibly three senior managers?"

Tom was in shock, but managed to say, "Thank you so much for the offer, may I have a day or two to give you my answer?"

Raymond then spoke for the first time.

"Tom, take a week to decide. We are all aware that you have just bought a house and you are quite settled."

Tom thanked them all and left in a bit of a daze.

The journey home would take an hour and a half and he spent that time thinking about how Ellen would take to the idea. When he got home he sat down and told Ellen what he had been offered. She was pleased for him but a little sad as it had taken them a long time to get back to Ipswich and they had just bought the house.

Ellen had always been supportive of Tom. Two hours later she went to Tom and said, "If its' something that you want, then we shall go. But, after we sell this house can we just rent somewhere until we are sure what the next move will be?"

Tom nodded his agreement.

"I think that this is sensible. Are you sure about the move?"

"Yes," said Ellen and kissed him.

Tom telephoned Tony to accept the offer to move to the North. The move was schedule to take place in three months so Ellen and Tom put the house on the market and made a couple of visits to the North. A month before the actual move they had a buyer in place for the house and they had found a nice rental house in Halifax.

On the day before the actual move Tom had rented a twenty one foot lorry which they loaded with all of their things. The house in Halifax was totally unfurnished. The next day Tom drove the lorry and Ellen drove Tom's car to Halifax. They left Ellen's car at her parents' house intending to collect it the next time they visited. The journey took just under three hours as the lorry was not as quick as a car and they arrived soon after twelve o' clock. The rest of the day was spent unpacking the lorry and, when that was done, Tom had to return the lorry to the local company.

Chapter 14

On the first day of work Tom met Raymond at his office which was in Manchester. Raymond had organized for Tom's three area managers to be there so he could introduce them. Raymond had given Tom the address and the drive from Halifax, along the M62, to Manchester took forty five minutes. He entered the office soon after nine o' clock and there was Raymond, two young men and a young lady.

"Welcome, Tom," Raymond said. "These are your three area managers. Allan, who has been with us for two years, Bob, who has been with us for eighteen months and Anita who has been with us for just six months."

All three said hello to Tom. One by one they told Tom which salons they were responsible for and gave Tom a briefing of each salon. The meeting, together with a short break for lunch, took most of the day. The last two hours of the meeting was used for Tom to make arrangements to meet them at certain salons and for the area manager to take Tom around to the salons they looked after but before that Tom had to go to America.

The company had an annual congress in Miami for divisional managers and above. Now that Tom was a division manager he was invited. The stay was for eleven days and was mostly for fun, beach volley ball and other games.

While Tom was there he met an expat from England who, ten years ago, had moved to America. He was now very high up the management scale, his name was Kevin. He said that he had heard of Tom and knew that Tony had put Tom's name forward for the Divisional Manager of the Year award.

Kevin then said to Tom, "I can give you a job as a divisional manager in San Francisco. It is a big unit taking over ten million dollars a year."

Tom thanked him and said that as soon as he got back home he would speak to Ellen. Kevin gave Tom his business card and Tom promised to call him with two days of Tom being home.

When Tom got home he discussed the America job with Ellen and she was keen to go. Tom called Kevin and accepted the job.

Tom telephoned Tony and told him about his conversation with Kevin. Tony already knew as Kevin was a friend of his and had spoken to Kevin who had told him about Tom. Tony said that that will be fine and he would write Tom out of the following years budget. Meanwhile Tom should carry on as usual.

The next couple of weeks were busy and Tom noticed that the salons in the North were pretty well run. He used his motivational powers as much as he could, mainly with the area managers but also with the salon managers as he met them.

Tom's previous salons in the South had won a retail competition from L'Oréal and the prize was a two day trip to Paris. Tom was invited. He drove down to Heathrow airport and met Raymond, Clive and three other divisional managers together with three people form L'Oréal.

On the plane Tom sat next to Stuart Williams who had been with L'Oréal for three years. They chatted about all sorts of things and Stuart asked Tom about children. Tom told him about his vasectomy and said any more children would not be possible.

"I had a vasectomy", Stuart said, "but had mine reversed. I now have two more children with my second wife."

This got Tom thinking.

The trip to Paris was busy visiting the Eifel Tower, not Tom's favorite place as all of the group went up. This was not good for Tom's fear of heights. They also went to the Louvre Museum, and the Notre Dame Cathedral. Tom thought the best trip was to have lunch on a boat going down the Seine.

When Tom retuned home he told Ellen about his conversation with Stuart regarding the reversal he had. They both agreed that they would go to a doctor in Manchester to discuss this with him. They were recommended to a doctor named John and made an appointment to see him.

They both sat in a reception of the doctor's and after three minutes were invited in. John explained what the procedure was and warned them that it was not always successful. Tom's age and the fact that his vasectomy was done thirteen years ago made chances of success poor. John sent them home to think about it.

When Tom and Ellen got home they discussed whether Tom should have the reversal.

"Why not," Tom said. "The worst that could happen is I get three days in bed."

Ellen agreed and they telephoned John and said they would like to go ahead. John made them an appointment for one week's time and gave Tom the address of the hospital.

Tom admitted himself into the hospital and the operation was scheduled for the following day. Ellen said she would visit the next afternoon. The following afternoon Ellen arrived looking concerned. Tom asked her what the problem was.

"I have just spoken to my father. My mother has had a heart attack. I am going to drive there now and I will be back to get you out of hospital tomorrow. Is that okay?"

"Of course. Don't worry about me, I will be fine. I am not allowed to move for the next two days so that the tubes will have a better chance to join."

Ellen left to go to Ipswich.

Two days later Ellen came to the hospital to collect Tom who was a little sore but otherwise fine. When they got in the car Tom asked Ellen, "How is your mum?"

"She is resting, but dad was scared he would lose her."

The next day Tom eased himself back into work, he was not going to let Tony or Raymond down. A week later Tom had to go back to the hospital to see if the operation was a success.

That evening John, the doctor, was going to phone them with the results. At six thirty the phone rang. Tom answered, it was John.

"Good news and bad news."

"Give me the bad news first please."

"There was not much of a sample."

Tom thought about this and remembered that they had made love the night before. He then said, "So, the good news?"

"It appears to have worked," John said.

Tom thanked him for everything, hung up the phone and told Ellen.

One week later Ellen hit Tom with a bombshell.

"I am sorry, Tom, but I cannot go to America. I am too worried about my mum."

"Don't worry, I can understand. I will go to London to speak to Tony tomorrow."

He then telephoned Tony to make an appointment to speak to him.

The next morning Tom drove down to London. Once he was seated he told Tony about Ellen's mother and that he could not go to America. Tony frowned.

"This is a problem. I have written you out of the budget for next year and already allocated your salons to other people. Of course, I will not have you unemployed and I can give you three salons in the north."

Tom thought on this. He then smiled and said, "Tony, I appreciate your gesture but you cannot afford my salary looking after three salons."

Tony nodded.

"The other alternative is we give you a 'golden handshake', say, ten thousand pounds."

Tom though for second and asked, "Tax free?"

"We can arrange this," Tony said.

"Thank you and thank you for giving me the opportunities that you have. I agree."

The meeting was over and Tom drove back to Halifax. Tony had spoken to Raymond who telephoned Tom that evening to wish him luck and said not to worry about work as he was sure that Tom would have lots of organizing to do.

The next day Ellen and Tom drove to Ipswich to go house hunting. They found a house on the same estate that they lived previously and put an offer in that day. The offer was accepted and they both then went to a Building Society to arrange a mortgage. Tom telephoned the solicitor that they used last time and gave him the details of the house and their contact detail in Halifax.

They spent four more weeks in Halifax, the sale was still not complete, and they put their furniture in storage. They then moved in to Ellen's parents' house. The sale was complete two weeks after this and Tom and Ellen drove to Halifax where Tom organized another twenty one foot lorry from the same company they used before.

They loaded the lorry and Tom drove this and Ellen her car. The company car had been returned. The furniture had to stay in the lorry overnight as they were to sign the completion contracts the next morning. Once they were signed and they had the keys, they unloaded the lorry and Tom returned it.

The next project was for Tom to find a job. Tom bought *The Daily Telegraph* to look for jobs. He saw one which appealed to him. It was for a management consulting company based in Kingston. He telephoned to get an appointment for an interview. His interview was arranged for the next day and he was given the address to go to. Tom used Ellen's car to get there and the journey around the M25 took ninety minutes.

Tom went into the offices, they were new and luxurious. The receptionist told him to take a seat and she would tell him when to go into the interview room. Five minutes later a man came out of a room and the receptionist told Tom to go into this room.

Tom entered and there was a man sitting behind a desk. The man stood up and offered his hand. Tom shook his hand.

"Hello. My name is Trevor Parker and you are Tom Levy, correct?"

Tom, smiled and said, "Yes, I am."

Trevor then asked Tom what he had been doing and some personal questions, married, children etc. Tom answered and gave Trevor his most recent background. After Tom had finished Trevor said, "The main interviews start next Monday, do you want to come?"

"Yes. I would like that."

With that, the interview was over and Tom drove back to Ipswich.

When Tom got home he told Ellen about the interview and how it went.

"I have a surprise for you," she said.

She was smiling so much Tom had to ask, "What?"

"I am pregnant."

Tom hugged her and said how pleased he was. Tom suggested a meal out to celebrate and Ellen agreed.

The following Monday Tom drove again to Kingston. When he got into the office there were many other men in the reception. A man came out of one of the office and asked for silence. He said, "My name is Lionel Spinks and I will be your trainer. Please go into that room and have a seat."

This he said pointing to a door. When they all entered it was placed out like a classroom. All of the men took a seat and Lionel took the front stage.

The day consisted of the men reading from a spreadsheet and some role play of how they would treat a managing director at the first meeting. At the end of the day Lionel said to the class, "Who would like to come back tomorrow?"

Everybody put their hands up. Lionel went out of the room and came back two minutes later. He called out three names and asked them to go to his office. When they had left he said to the rest of the people, "I will see you all tomorrow."

Tom drove home, told Ellen about his day, ate early and went to bed, exhausted. The next day followed a similar pattern to the previous one, this time how to read a P&L and again with some role play. At the end of the day Lionel called out three names who went to his office and were never seen again.

This process went on all week and there was only Tom and another man left. He introduced himself as George Spencer and it appeared that only Tom and George had got the job. Because of this, George and Tom became friends.

The job involved receiving a phone call on the Sunday night and being told where to go at an appointed time the next day. This could be in the far north of the country or the far south. How they got there was their problem, train, car or airplane. They had strict instructions to only travel first class and arrive at exactly the time that they were supposed to. Lionel told them that it was rude to be late and only salesmen arrived early. So, if their appointment was for seven in the morning they should wait outside till exactly seven before they entered.

When they were in the company they were to interview the managing director for two hours and then interview the senior staff. When they got back to their hotel rooms they were to go through the P&L and the balance sheet of the company. At the end of their time in the company they would have another meeting with the managing director and make recommendation as to how to improve the company.

Most times they would be away for the week, not getting home till Friday. If, for example, they finished their first company on the Tuesday, they would get instruction to go to another company on the Wednesday, this could be the other side of the country.

As demanding as it was, Tom loved it. His first few companies were small. He called these his 'garage businesses'. To explain this, his example was a good garage mechanic decided to open his own business. He knew nothing about accounts, marketing, pricing etc. So, he was still a good mechanic but needed someone like Tom to help him with the business side.

With the larger companies it was sometimes even easier. They had the answers if they spoke to their staff who were always helpful to Tom. Tom repeated the suggestions that the senior staff made and the managing director was impressed.

After Tom had been doing this for two weeks, one Friday he went home and Ellen was upset. She told him that she had lost the baby. He tried to put a positive spin on this telling her that at least they knew the reversal had worked. Within two months she was pregnant again.

Both Tom and George progressed to the larger companies, some taking over a million pounds a year. Nine months later Ellen had her first child. It was a boy and they named him Toby. With another four months after Toby was borne Ellen was pregnant again.

Tom was earning quite good money and, in spite of the travelling and the stress he was still enjoying his job. This changed when Ellen gave birth to their daughter which they name Zoe. He missed watching his children grow up.

He kept in touch with his first son, Julien, who occasionally came to stay but, as Julien was in his early twenties he had his own life.

This life was now in Ireland, which is where Jenny had moved to.

Tom told Ellen that he was going to leave the management consultancy company because he did not want to spend all of the week away. Ellen asked him what he would do.

"I don't know but I will find something."

Chapter 15

As Tom was now forty four this did not prove as easy as he thought it would. He struggled to even get an interview. Eventually he saw an advert for a marketing manager in Walton on Thames. He telephoned and got an interview. He was to meet at a hairdressing salon named Angelo's and was to meet Angelo himself.

He arrived at the appointed time and went into the salon. The salon was beautifully done with bespoke furniture. Angelo explained the job needed which was selling a a computerized hair colouring system developed by a company named Redbow. The computer screen was 'touch screen' and after entering information, such as the amount of grey hair the client had, the client's natural colour and the desired colour, the computer would tell you what products to mix. It was revolutionary.

Tom told Angelo he loved it and Angelo said he could start working as soon as he wanted. Tom's basic salary was not good but the commission on sales of the system was good. Tom went home and told Ellen all about his conversation with Angelo.

"I think it sounds good," she said, "but the travelling everyday will be a nightmare. Why don't we sell the house and rent something nearer? You need to work as we have four mouths to feed so the job is more important."

Tom was impressed as to how supportive Ellen was.

Tom rented a house in Sunbury on Thames, a ten minute drive from the salon, and Ellen stayed in Ipswich until the house was sold.

The idea that Angelo had was to sell the computerized colouring system, which could only be used with Redbow products, and he would get a commission from Redbow for selling their colours.

Tom worked long and hard but it was not easy to get salons to change the hair colours that they were used to using. In the first two months they had only sold two systems, this effected Tom's income. Another month went buy and Ellen joined Tom in Sunbury on Thames.

Tom met Gino, the managing director of Redbow, and got on well. He later met Roberto, Gino's brother who had opened up Redbow in America.

They struggled through for another year not selling too many systems and Tom realized that because of Angelo's lack of financial it was not going to be a success. Most of their savings had gone supplementing the poor salary that Tom was getting. Tom decided that he would leave.

Tom told Angelo, who was disappointed, but understood. He too was disillusioned with the project. The day after Tom told Angelo he received a telephone call from Gino. Gino told Tom to come and see him to his factory in Islington.

Tom went to Islington and found where Gino's factory was. Gino saw Tom and walked towards him to greet him. Both men shook hands and Gino invited Tom into his office. Once seated Gino said with a thick Italian accent, "So, you want to leave Angelo. What do you plan to do?"

"I do not know. I loved Angelo, and his family, but I have two children myself to feed and, as much as it hurts me to say it, I cannot see Angelo being successful."

Gino thought for a moments and then said, "How much do you need to live on?"

Tom thought for moment, he pretty well knew, and told Gino a figure. Gino nodded.

"You have too much experience to lose. I want you to come and work for me here. What do you think?"

Tom was not only surprised, but delighted, at his age it would not be easy to find a job.

"I would like that very much," he said, "thank you for your offer."

They agreed a start date, which was three days time, shook hands and Tom left to give the good news to Ellen.

Tom took public transport to Islington leaving Ellen the car, she had two kids to transport around. When Tom arrived at Gino's he met the other staff. There was Maurice, the accountant, and Theresa, Gino's sister. He later met Mario who was the production manage and later on he met Bob who did the installation of the salon furniture. Tom didn't know about the salon furniture but soon found out.

As well as making hair colour Gino also fitted out hair salons with bespoke furniture. The furniture was custom made in Italy, transported back to England and Bob would install it.

Gino adopted Tom and treated him like a son. Tom did everything he could to repay Gino. Tom even developed a new skill. He taught himself to use the computer and bought a 'cad' programme and started to use this to design salon. He would go to the empty shop, meet the owner and take measurements. Then he would go back to his desk and design the salon and then meet the owner to discuss the design. If the owner was happy, Tom would put the order in for the furniture.

As the years went on Tom became quite well known for this and salon owners asking for him. Gino, who used to do the designs on paper left this department totally to Tom. Tom knew to leave one point three meters between electric sockets, that was the space needed for hairdresser to work next to each other.

After Tom had been with Gino for eighteen months Gino bought him a company car, it was a little Fiat. Six months later Tom went with Gino to Sweden to demonstrate the hair colour. It was a company that wanted Redbow to make colour for them using their packaging. They met the managing director and he asked if Tom could do a demonstration of the colour. Gino said he could.

In another part of the building there was a salon set up and four models were seated ready to have their hair coloured. Tom talked to the models asking what colour they would like and the managing director, whose name was Heinrich, had staff to apply the hair colour under Tom's instruction.

Fortunately, the colours came out well and Heinrich was delighted. He wanted Gino and Tom to come to his house the next day and, as Gino and Tom were sleeping in the guest room in the factory, he said he would collect them at ten o clock.

At ten o clock the next day Heinrich came to the factory in his Rolls Royce. Tom and Gino got in and Heinrich said they were going to his house and on to his boat and go down the canal.

When they arrived at his house they went in and straight through to the kitchen and out the rear door. There was a small lawn that led down to the canal and moored to a small jetty was Heinrich's boat. It was a small motor boat, enough room for six people.

The three of them got on the boat and Heinrich started the motor and set off down the canal. The boat ride was peaceful and after thirty minutes Heinrich opened some champagne and vodka. The next two hours were spent cruising along on the river and drinking champagne and vodka.

They arrived back at Heinrich's house as the sun was setting. Part of the conversation on the boat was about food and Gino offered to do a traditional spaghetti Bolognaise. Once in the house Gino took over the kitchen and Tom and Heinrich played snooker on a full sized table.

Within an hour they had all eaten and Heinrich suggested they all have a sauna. His sauna could house six people. They stayed for one more hour and then Heinrich took them back to the factory to their guests room. After waking the next morning, Tom and Gino had a light breakfast of cheese and cold meats and they organized a taxi to take them to the airport for their flight home.

The following week after that when Tom was home Ellen made some food and sat down with him.

"We still have the money for a deposit and you are earning quite good money, how do you feel about moving back to Ipswich?"

Tom could see that this was important to her.

"If you want to, it's fine with me, but I am afraid you will have to go and look at properties. I have to go to France with Gino and very soon after that I have to go to Las Vegas."

Ellen was pleased and said to leave everything to her.

A week later Gino took Tom to France to demonstrate the colouring system and they spent two days there. Two weeks after that they both went to Las Vegas, met Roberto, Gino's brother, and spent two days in an exhibition centre doing more demonstrations.

When Tom got home Ellen was very excited, she had found a house that she liked and they could afford in Ipswich. Tom agreed to go that weekend to have a look at it. They packed the children into the car and set off for Ipswich to view the house.

The house was in Kensington Gardens just off of the Norwich Road, probably a ten minute walk to the centre of town. All four of them went in to view the house which was detached.

Inside was large with large entrance hall. It needed some decoration and the rooms were filled with old furniture. When they had seen all of the house the four of them got back into the car waiting to hear what the others would say. Ellen was first to speak.

"What do we all think?"

The children said they loved it. Tom smiled and said, "I love it too. Lets' tell the agents that we want to buy it."

Everybody in the car cheered.

Tom and Ellen bought the house and Gino was surprised. Tom would have to travel ninety minutes each way to get to work. To avoid the traffic Tom left home soon after six and arrived in Islington by seven thirty. He then went to a local café after buying a newspaper, mainly for the crosswords, and had breakfast. He was at his office by eight thirty.

When Tom had been with Gino for eleven years Gino's son joined the company. He had no personality and took a dislike to Tom as he had become so close to his father. Tom was doing less and less work as Gino was letting his son run the company. This was the most miserable that Tom had been for the last ten years.

When he went home and complained to Ellen her only comment was, why not leave. This generally led to an argument with Tom asking, who would buy the food and pay the mortgage. Tom was now forty seven years old and almost unemployable. The relationship with Ellen deteriorated.

One year later Tom arrived home and Ellen told him she wanted a divorce, she had met somebody else. They argued a little that night and Ellen went out and didn't return till the next day. Tom couldn't go to work as he had to stay and keep the children safe.

The atmosphere between them was pretty bad, but after one week they started to talk. Tom asked who she had met and she told him that her first ever boyfriend had found her on Facebook and started to contact her. One thing led to another.

Tom had been sleeping on the settee since Ellen went out for the night. When he got to work he spoke to Gino. Gino was not happy.

"But you moved to Ipswich for her!"

Gino added that he had a friend who had a flat to rent and he would speak to him. Tom thanked him.

It turned out that the friend that Gino knew was Mario. The production manager. He told Tom he could have the flat for one month without charge, knowing the circumstances, and after that, if Tom didn't find somewhere else he would have to charge him the full rent. Tom thanked him and on his next journey to Ipswich he gathered his clothes and personal items to takeback to Mario's flat.

Tom still knew how to play bridge and he started to go to two local clubs. He was a good player and got on well with the people there and made some friends. One of the players he played with was named Robert and after listening to Tom's story Robert said he had a small house to rent in Chigwell. He said that he house was empty and needed a coat of paint everywhere but he would give Tom a month's free rent to decorate it. Tom accepted and the next day Robert gave him the address and keys to the house.

JP, Gino's son, made contact with a South African company who wanted to be the agents for Redbow, selling Redbow products throughout South Africa. He took frequent trips there and the mood at work lightened when he did.

One day at the office somebody told Tom that there was somebody on line two wanting technical help. Tom picked up line two and said, "Tom Levy, how can I help you?"

A female voice replied, "I am having a problem using your Crazy Color, can you help?"

Tom asked her what the problem was and she told him the colour didn't come out as she expected. Tom asked her a few questions, what is your natural hair colour, do you have any grey hair etc. She answered his questions and, based on her answers, Tom gave her the solution. Tom then said to her he would like to send her a free box, what was her address. She gave Tom the address and then said, "I am sure you have never heard of Eastcote."

Tom laughed.

"I used to work there. Field End Road."

"Where about in Field End Road?" asked Laura, the lady on the other end of the phone.

Tom told her the agency where he worked.

"Mr. Cohen is my landlord. Shall I tell him I have spoken to you?"

"If you do he will probably put your rent up. Our last meeting did not go too well," Tom said, half jokingly.

Laura said okay and Tom said he would send the free box of Crazy Color out today and the call ended.

Two days later Laura telephoned and asked to speak to Tom. Tom picked up line two, he was told who was on the phone and expected she was ringing to thank him for the colour he had sent.

"Hello Laura, did you get the colour?"

"I did, thank you, but that is not while I am calling. I did tell Mr. Cohen that we had spoken and he asked me for your contact details. Do you mind if I give them to him?"

Tom was in shock and did not know what to say. Eventually he said, "No, that will be fine, just tell him it is my work number."

Laura said she would and the conversation ended there.

The next day Maurice telephoned the company and asked to speak to Tom. Theresa, who had answered the call yelled across the office to Tom.

"There is a Mr. Cohen on the line for you Tom. Line three."

Tom decided to just be light with the conversation. He picked up the phone.

"Hello Maurice, how are you?"

"I am fine, thank you, Tom, how are you?"

The both chatted away with Tom telling Maurice where the office was and where he was living.

"How would you like to meet for some lunch?" Maurice said.

"That would be great. I would like that."

Maurice suggested a restaurant in town and it was arranged for the following Tuesday at midday. Tom replaced the handset and just stared ahead of himself not knowing what to make of this. He was pleased as Maurice had always been good to him and he thought it sad that Maurice felt betrayed.

Chapter 16

Every evening when Tom finished work he went straight to the house and painted. He normally spent between two to three hours before he went back to Mario's flat. On Saturday mornings he drove to Ipswich to watch his son, Toby, play rugby.

The relationship between Ellen and himself had improved and they had even become friends with one common aim, to make sure the children didn't suffer because of them separating. Tom also became more philosophical understanding that the age difference would eventually come to this. After all, Tom was nearing sixty and she was still in her late thirties.

On the Monday, after work, Tom went to the house to paint. He only had two weeks free rent left and realized that the six hundred pounds a month, although manageable, would mean he had very little to contribute to Ellen to bring up the children. He decided that he would need to find somebody to share the house with and also share the expenses. He decided that on Wednesday he would put an advert in the local papers.

Tuesday morning Tom was nervous. It had been more than twenty years since he had last spoke to Maurice. He went to the restaurant and arrived fifteen minutes early so he waited outside. Ten minutes later Maurice was walking towards him.

They both shook hands and said hello.

"I have booked a table," Maurice said. "Come on, let's go in."

Tom followed Maurice who was obviously a regular because he was greeted by 'Hello Mr. Cohen'. They were led to a table and they both sat down.

After ordering and throughout the meal they talked for one hour, about absolutely nothing. Their football teams, the state of the government and anything but what had happened or what had happened over the last twenty years. At the end of the meal Tom thanked Maurice and Maurice said we must do this again.

"Do you have a home phone number?" He then asked Tom.

"Within the next two weeks I am moving into a small house in Chigwell. When I do I shall organize a phone then," replied Tom.

Maurice gave Tom a business card.

"When you do, call me and give me the number. How do you feel about lunch again next Tuesday?"

Tom said that would be great and they arranged to meet at this restaurant at the same time next week. Tom then left to go back to work.

When Tom got back to the office JP approached him.

"In two weeks I am going back to South Africa because the company have taken a stand in an exhibition. I would like you to come with me to demonstrate the computerized colouring system. Will that be okay?"

Tom said that would be fine and asked the details, what day will they go and for how long. JP told him they would fly out on the Tuesday and they would be away for five days.

On Wednesday Tom put the advert in for a 'house sharer'. The paper was to come out the next day and as long as Tom got his advert to the papers before twelve his advert would be in the next day's paper. Tom had to use the office telephone number for contact and Gino said this would be fine.

At ten thirty the next day Maurice, the accountant, called over to Tom and said there was a call for him on line one. Tom picked up the phone.

"Hello, this is Tom Levy, can I help you?"

"You are advertising for a house share, is it still available?" a male voice on the other end of the line said.

"Yes."

"My name is Danny," said the man on the other end of the phone. "Can we meet to look at the house?"

"Of course, but I am still decorating it and have no furniture yet."

Danny said he did not mind and, after Tom gave Danny the address, they arranged to meet at 6 o clock that evening.

Tom got to the house at ten to six and ten minutes later the doorbell rang. Tom opened the door and Tom assumed it was Danny. He was roughly thirty years old with blonde curly hair.

"Danny?"

"Yes," said Danny, smiling.

Tom opened the door wider and Danny stepped in. They walked around the house, the painting was almost finished, and Danny looked at all the rooms.

"When are you going to move in and what is the monthly rent?" Danny asked.

"I want to move in not this weekend but the next one. I shall finish the painting in the next couple of days and, on Saturday, I am going shopping for furniture, a cooker and a fridge, freezer. The rent is three hundred pounds a month each and we shall share the bills with the exception of property rates, the landlord will pay this."

"That will be fine," Danny said. "If its' okay I will move in on the same day."

Tom said it was. They talked on for another hour and Tom was pleased that Danny supported the same football team as Tom. They got on really well.

"Do you want company when you go shopping on Saturday?" asked Danny.

"That will be great. How about I meet you here at ten o' clock?"

Danny said that would be great. They shook hands and Danny left. Tom did some more painting.

Tom was only able to shop for furniture on Saturday because Toby's rugby match had been arranged for Sunday. Tom met Danny at ten o' clock on the Saturday and they went to look for a second hand cooker and fridge. Fortunately, Danny had brought his car which was a station wagon and both of them fitted into the back. Danny needed a station wagon because he was a window cleaner and needed to carry ladders on the roof. They then went to a cheap furniture shop and bought two beds, a settee which could turn into a bed if one of the kids wanted to stay and two small 'flat pack' wardrobes. Tom told Danny that he would look during the week for a second hand table and chairs as money was getting tight.

Danny and Tom took the cooker and the fridge back to the house and unloaded them. They then went back to the furniture shop to collect their flat packed furniture. When everything was deposited into the house they went to the supermarket and bought six beers which they took back to the house to celebrate.

Tom then told Danny that could move in on Saturday morning but he would be going to Ipswich on the Sunday as his son's rugby team had their annual family 'get together'.

The following day, Sunday, Tom drove to Ipswich to watch Toby playing. He stood on the touchline with Ellen and their daughter Zoe. They were so proud that Toby was playing in a league match. Unfortunately, Toby's team lost. Ellen asked Tom if he wanted to come back for a bite to eat but Tom told her about the house and his new 'housemate' and said he should go back. He thanked her for the invitation and drove back to Chigwell.

On the following Monday Danny telephoned Tom at work and said he had found second hand table and four chairs for eight ponds and he asked Tom if he should buy them Tom said yes and he would give him the money back that evening.

On Tuesday Tom met Maurice for lunch and they talked about their old times together and laughed at their old jokes like there had been no intermittent time.

Danny met Tom on Friday after work and they went to the cheapest place they could find to buy bedclothes, towels and anything else they would need. Tom and Danny were becoming close friends. Saturday was spent erecting the 'flat fold' furniture positioning where the fridge should go and generally making the house good enough for them to live in.

Danny said he would cook and they went to the local supermarket and bought food. Tom added a bottle of wine to their shopping. The evening they both spent eating, laughing and drinking.

On Sunday Tom drove to Ipswich and met Ellen and Zoe by the side of the pitch. The annual family 'get together' was that everyone, including parents, played baseball. Tom's team were first to take the field as fielders, the other team were to bat first. After twenty minutes somebody gave a mighty hit towards Tom and he chased it going backwards to try to catch it. He made three backward strides and there was a huge pain in his left leg and he collapsed. Tom couldn't move without pain so he just lay there.

Everybody came towards him and somebody called an ambulance. He was taken to hospital and Ellen and the two children followed in Ellen's car. When the ambulance arrived at the hospital, Tom was taken on a wheeled stretcher inside. Ellen and the children went to the waiting room.

After an hour Tom emerged on crutches and told them all that his hamstring had torn and besides that there was no problem. Ellen asked him how he was going to get back to Chigwell and Tom told her that fortunately Gino had bought him an automatic and he only needed his right leg.

After kissing the kids Tom drove back to Chigwell, more in discomfort than pain. As long as he kept his left leg straight, it was well strapped up, he was fine driving. Whilst driving back he remembered his next problem. In two days time he was to fly to South Africa. When Tom arrived at the house and used his crutches to go in Danny laughed and teased him.

On the Monday morning when Tom arrived at work he walked into the office on his crutches. Everybody in the office came towards him asking, what happened, how did you do it, are you okay? Tom told the gathering crowd what had happened and said he was fine. He went to his desk to continue what he had been doing since JP took over the business, nothing.

After a few minutes JP approached Tom's desk and sat opposite him.

"Will you still be able to come to South Africa?"

"I can stand, I can speak, I can demonstrate, the only problem may be the plane, walking up the stairs to get on."

"I will phone the airport and see what can be done."

With that JP left Tom's desk.

One hour later JP came back to Tom's desk and sat down again.

"I have spoken to the airport and they said it will be no problem, they often have people with disabilities and they can cater for you. When we get to the airport I will check us in and go to 'Airport Support' and they will arrange everything. Maybe, under the circumstance, I should drive us both there. Our plane takes off at nine in the evening so we shall have plenty of time. Are you okay with that?"

Tom said that would be fine and JP left.

Tom remembered his regular lunch date with Maurice and telephoned him to cancel. He told Maurice he was on crutches and it would be difficult to get to the restaurant. Maurice, with his usual sense of humour, said that Tom could now do Long John Silver in pantomime. Tom promised to call him when he got back from South Africa.

Tom knew that JP wanted to leave early so he had bought clothes for four days to the office. At five JP help Tom into his car and they set off for Heathrow airport.

Traffic was heavy, it was rush hour, and they got to the airport in two hours. JP went into the airport for assistants and somebody came out with a wheelchair. Tom sat in it and the man that brought the wheelchair out started pushing it when Tom was seated in it. JP followed them.

When the three of them got into the airport Tom and JP were rushed through security and customs and were led to their gate. It was only seven fifteen. JP was not known for his sense of humour, but he tried to be funny and said to Tom, "I should take a cripple more often, I have never got through that lot so quickly."

He laughed at his own joke.

Forty minutes before they were due to take off a man came and took Tom's wheelchair just outside the airport. He pushed the chair towards a waiting van. When they got to the back of the van a hydraulic ramp came down and Tom's chair was pushed onto it and in the van. The rear door was closed and the van started to move. Three minutes later the van stopped by a plane.

The hydraulic ramp went down and Tom was pushed out of the van onto another ramp. Once Tom's chair was secured this ramp started to lift up to the plane's door. Tom's chair was then pushed onto the plane. Tom was given the front seat which had the most 'leg room'. Sometime later, JP came and sat next to him.

At nine o' clock the plane took off. Thirty minutes later drinks were served and at ten thirty a good meal was served. There was a film showing at eleven thirty and after that the lights were turned down for people to sleep. The plane started to descend after eleven and a half hours in the air and they landed close to twelve, one hour after takeoff. It was now ten thirty in the evening in South Africa.

When the plane stopped all of the passengers got off, including JP. They got Tom off of the plane the same way as they got him on, through hydraulic lifts. Tom was wheeled through customs and was taken to the main concourse and the man wheeling him waited for JP to arrive. JP was about to push Tom in the wheelchair and Tom said he would walk if JP would pass him his crutches.

They walked out of the airport and JP hailed a taxi. He told the driver which hotel to go to. When they arrived outside the hotel Tom could see it was a high class one. The driver took their bags out of the boot of the car and immediately somebody from the hotel staff collected them and took them into the foyer following JP.

JP checked in, he had already made the reservation, and both Tom and himself were given plastic keys. It was almost midnight now. They both went to their rooms to try and have some sleep.

Tom slept little as he had had a good sleep on the plane but he managed to doze until six. At eight o clock he made his was down the restaurant to meet JP for breakfast.

After breakfast Tom and JP got a taxi to the South African company which was named 'Black Like Me'. They were met by the managing director, who introduced himself to Tom.

"Hello, Tom. My name is Martin Osure and welcome to both my company and my country."

The schedule was for Tom to stand on stage and lecture Martin's staff on the Computerised Colouring System. There were twelve people sitting in what can only described as a classroom.

Tom was to spend the morning demonstrating the system and in the afternoon Black Like Me had organized some models to have their hair coloured. Tom had to be careful as the models' hair was a different texture to what he had been used to.

The next two days were to be spent at a hairdressing exhibition demonstrating the Colouring System. The only thing that Tom found strange was that the taxi that took them to the exhibition insisted that all the cabs doors were locked when they went through the Townships.

For Tom, the two days were pretty exhausting. Standing for long hours supported by his crutches which made his underarms very sore but he managed to survive. He spent many hours talking to salon owners explain the benefits of using the system.

Finally on day four Tom and JP were ready to go home. JP complimented Tom on what a good job he had done. This did not change their relationship, but it made Tom's job more bearable.

Tom played bridge three to four nights a week. He made a number of good friends, two female friends being the closest. Whenever either of these two ladies needed a partner for an event Tom was chosen. There was no sexual attraction for any of them but they became close as friends.

One evening Sandra, one of these two ladies, invited Tom for a meal before they went to bridge.

After they had eaten Sandra said. "It is about time you took yourself away from bridge and found a nice lady to spend some time with."

Tom smiled.

"I have more faith in the bridge table than I have in relationships. Thanks, but I will stick to bridge."

Sandra was not deterred.

"There is a nice dating site that I have used, why don't you go on it?"

"Sandra, firstly I cannot afford it, secondly I could not afford to take somebody out and thirdly, I had a good twenty years with Ellen but I am not sure I want to go through it again."

Sandra, who was quite a wealthy lady then said. "I'll do a deal with you. I will pay to put you on the site and I will write the information. All you have to do is to receive the calls, Okay?"

Tom knew that there was no point in arguing with Sandra so he agreed. She made him stand against the wall while she took a picture of him. Soon after that they both went to the bridge club and Tom forgot all about it.

Three months earlier Redbow were throwing out an old computer, it still worked, so Tom asked if he could have it and JP said he could. Because he now had a computer at home he had broadband installed added to his phone line.

Four days after the conversation with Sandra about internet dating Tom received three emails from ladies suggesting that they meet. He replied to these emails saying he preferred to speak on the phone to sending emails and asked these ladies for their telephone number. After receiving the emails Tom thought it best if he looked up the profile that Sandra had made for him. Most of it was true, his hobbies, his likes, his dislike etc., but Sandra had put Tom's age down as fifty one, or he was fifty nine.

All three replied with their mobile phone numbers. Tom didn't have a mobile phone and decided to get either a cheap one or a second hand one.

At work the next day, Tom was still doing very little and he went out and found a second hand electrical shop. In the shop was an old Nokia phone for fifteen pounds so he bought it. He then went to Vodafone shop and bought a 'pay as you go' Sim card.

When he was home that evening he telephoned one of the ladies that had sent him the email. After three rings the phone was answered.

"Hello, Barbara speaking."

"Hello, this is Tom."

Barbara's voice lightened up.

"Hello Tom, thank you for calling."

They chatted for a few minutes and Barbara lived locally to Tom and they arranged to meet the next day in a pub which was only a four minute walk for Tom.

The next evening Tom went to the pub to meet Barbara. He had seen her picture on the dating site so he knew what she looked like.

As he entered the pub he saw her sitting at a table. Tom went to the table.

"Hello Barbara, would you like a drink?"

She had one in front of her so she replied, "No, I am fine with this one, thank you?"

Barbara had what you might call a Rubenesque figure, plump. Tom immediately did not feel attracted to her, but he stayed chatting to her for one hour. She could feel that Tom was not interested and she thanked him for coming, he also thanked her, and they parted company.

The next day he contacted the second lady on his list and telephoned her. Her name was Susan. They arranged to meet, but this date had the same effect as the first one. In the meantime Tom received two more emails from ladies wanting to meet. He exchanged telephone numbers with them.

Tom contacted the third lady on his original list, her name was Jill. He telephoned her.

The phone rang twice and Jill answered saying, quite gruffly, "Hello."

"Hello Jill, this is Tom."

Jill started shouting down the phone.

"Why did you wait three days to contact me? This is not the way to treat someone. I don't think I want to meet you."

Tom thought she was crazy and just said, "Fine." And disconnected the phone.

Tom's Bridge games cost him one pound a night, but this dating was costing him much more, so he decided that he would have a week off. Three days later Tom received a call from Jill.

"I have been thinking about you and I would now like to meet you."

Tom's initial reaction was to cut the call, but he had never been rude to a lady.

"When and where?" he asked.

She suggested the following evening and at a coffee shop in Golders Green.

"Okay," Tom said.

When Tom told Danny about the conversation they both had a good laugh. Danny asked Tom if he would like him to follow then in case she was a 'bunny boiler', referring to the film, *Fatal Attraction*. Tom laughed but said he would make sure that they were always in public places and never in dark alleys.

Danny had become a good friend, but Tom was aware of his problem, he drank too much and seeing him sober was rare. Tom became like a father to Danny, budgeting out his money and taking a certain amount each week so Danny kept up with the rent payments. Danny, who was a window cleaner, was always paid in cash and if Tom didn't take his money he would spend it on drink. Danny was happy with this arrangement.

The following evening Tom drove to Golders Green and went to the coffee shop that he had arranged to meet Jill. She was already sat at a table, Tom joined her. She was more attractive than her profile picture on the dating site.

After chatting for an hour Jill said to Tom, "Would you like to come back to my house for a glass of wine?"

"That would be nice," Tom replied, "do you live far away?"

Jill said it was a three minute walk and he could leave his car where he had parked it.

Tom paid for the coffees and then followed Jill out of the shop. She was correct, three minutes later she took out her keys and opened a front door. Tom followed her in. He didn't get the wine but within one minute he was in her bedroom. Two hours later Tom left and went back to his car.

Tom and Jill's relationship lasted three weeks, Tom had removed himself from the dating website. After three weeks Tom decided that Jill had an emotional problem. Without provocation she would fly into a fit of rage and then apologise.

The last fit of rage went on for an hour and Tom said, "Goodbye, Jill. Enough is enough."

With that he walked out of the house for the last time.

Things over the next few weeks went well, work was the same, boring, he enjoyed meeting Maurice for lunch on Tuesday and he was doing well in the bridge club. One evening, when not playing bridge, Tom sat and chatted to Danny. He told Danny, although some of the dates were a pain, he quite missed them.

"Why not go back on the site. You know who to avoid."

Danny laughed at his own joke. Tom said he would and reinstated his profile that Sandra had created for him.

Within the next two days Tom received three invitations. He made contact with these ladies and exchanged telephone numbers. He then rechecked his profile again and remembered the false age that Sandra had put down. Tom was not good at lying, he thought to be a good liar you had to have a good memory. When talking on his past dates he had to carefully work out Julien's age, and calculate so it matched with his false age.

Tom telephoned the three ladies he was in touch with and told them his real age. He then told them to think about this and call him if they were still interested.

 One of the ladies whose name was Ellen called the next day and said she would still like to meet if he wanted to. Tom said yes. He told her where he lived and she said she knew it as her parents use to live close bye. They agreed to meet the next day and Ellen said she would pick Tom up at the corner of his road.

The next day, at six thirty, Tom stood on the corner of his road. Ellen stopped her little red car and Tom got in. He leaned across and pecked her on the cheek. Ellen drove to a pub which was only a few minutes away and when they entered, she took a seat and Tom went to order drink, Ellen had already told him what she would like.

Tom took the drinks back to where Ellen was sitting and they started to talk. Tom found out that Ellen had been married twice and she had two daughters, one from one husband and the other from another husband. She and her first husband split up fifteen years ago and she had split up from her second husband four years ago. She told Tom that she was still friends with her first husband but not the second. Tom asked her what made her decide to come for the date.

"I knew that your picture profile was not false as you play bridge at the same club my sister plays and she told me that your picture was real."

They both laughed at this.

Tom gave her a brief resume of his life and, before they knew it, the pub announced it was closing. Before they left the pub Tom asked, "Would you like to come to my house for a meal on Saturday, I will try to keep my house mate sober."

They both laughed at Tom's last remark.

"Yes, I would like that. What time?"

Tom told her six thirty. The both went to the car for Ellen to drive Tom back. When they arrived at the corner of Tom's road, Tom leaned over and gave Ellen a peck on the cheek. Ellen looked at Tom and passionately kissed him back.

Thirty seconds later Tom opened his front door. Danny was still awake and watching the television that Tom had rented a month ago. Tom told Danny about his evening and about making a meal on Saturday.

"If you like I will cook my specialty, spaghetti bolognaise," Danny said.

Tom smiled. Danny had invited himself.

"That sounds great, she is coming at six thirty."

The next day Ellen telephoned Tom and asked if she could bring her daughter on Saturday.

"No problem," Tom said. "Looking forward to seeing you."

On Saturday afternoon Danny was busy cooking. Tom spent the time cleaning and preparing the table.

Ellen and her daughter arrived at six thirty. Tom welcomed them both in.

"This is my daughter, Angela."

"Hello, please come in. Let me get you young ladies a drink."

The evening went well and nobody suffered from food poisoning. At nine o clock Ellen said she should go home. Angela thanked

Tom and Danny for the meal and Tom told her she was welcome.

As the girls were leaving there was a tender kiss from Ellen to Tom.

"Maybe you could come to my house and let me cook for you," she said.

Tom smiled.

"I would like that very much."

They arranged for the next Saturday when both the girls were to spend the weekend with their fathers. Ellen gave Tom her address and said she would see him at six thirty.

Tom was very nervous when he arrived at Ellen's house on the Saturday. For a long time, he had not felt an emotion like he was feeling now. Ellen opened the door to let Tom in and they both had a passionate kiss. She grabbed his hand and gently pulled him into the house.

The house was a large three bedroomed semi detached house. Tom saw that in the back garden there was a large swimming pool. The kitchen was together with a dining room attached and Tom went and sat at the table in the dining room.

Ellen served a Sunday roast with chicken and they both started to eat. They spent the next two hours talking about their pasts. At nine thirty Ellen took Tom's hand and led him upstairs.

There was none of the franticness and they spent many hours just loving each other.

When Tom woke the next morning he gently let himself out of bed. He looked down and Ellen was still sleeping. He went down to the kitchen and looked for coffee. By the time Tom found the coffee Ellen came downstairs. She gently kissed him and showed him where the coffee was.

Tom felt something special was happening between him and Ellen and there was a tingling inside him. They had coffee and Ellen asked what Tom would like for breakfast.

"I would really like just some toast, is that okay?"

Ellen smiled.

"Whatever you want."

They spent the rest of the day going for a walk in the local park and then lunch at the pub they first met. Ellen insisted on paying, much to Tom's relief as he was not sure how much money he had.

In the afternoon Ellen said that she was very happy and she hoped that he was.

"It is a long time since I have felt so happy," Tom replied.

Chapter 17

Work was the usual boring thing with Tom spending a lot of time playing Solitaire and trying to find things to do. His relationship with Ellen was growing stronger. He had met her youngest daughter, Anita, who was not particularly friendly but was polite.

After three weeks Ellen told Tom that she had arranged a holiday in Egypt with her sister, Sharon. She asked him if he would move in and keep an eye on her daughters. Tom said that he would.

Tom took Ellen and Sharon to the airport. He kissed Ellen goodbye and told Sharon how pleased he was to meet her. After saying to then both 'have a nice holiday', he went back to Ellen's house.

Both Ellen's children were pleasant and looking after them was not difficult. The week was not too tough. Tom had arranged to collect Ellen and Sharon from the airport and he arrived at Stanstead airport early. The girls came through the departures gate looking tanned and happy. He took Sharon home first and then took Ellen home.

When they got home Ellen hugged bother girls. Tom had prepared a stew for them all to eat and, when Ellen unpacked they all sat down to eat. The girls went to their rooms to do their homework and Ellen and Tom sat together on the settee in the lounge.

"Why don't you move in with me here, I miss you when you are not here?" Ellen said to Tom.

Tom was worried that this might be too soon, but replied, "I would like that, if you are sure?"

Ellen said she was.

Tom went back to his house and found Danny there, not too sober. He told Danny to sit down on the settee. Once Danny was seated he said to Danny, "Ellen has asked me to move in with her. I don't know how it will work out but thought you should know."

Danny's brain was already murky due to the amount of drink he had had but managed to say, "I am pleased for you."

"There are three weeks left before the rent is due and hopefully I will know whether this will work out. If it does, I will give you another month to find somebody to share the house with, okay?"

Danny, who couldn't calculate a week, let alone a month said, "That will be fine. I am pleased for you."

He slurred.

Tom moved his things to Ellen's house and officially moved in. Ellen and Tom were very happy and life, with the exception of Tom's work, was good. After seven weeks Tom told Danny that he was moving out and Danny would have to find somebody else to share the house with. Danny said, "okay".

After two months Ellen asked Tom how work was going.

"You don't talk much about it," she said.

Tom decided to tell her the truth, starting with time with Gino and now to the present. It took almost an hour and Ellen listened intently. She said she sympathized with him.

Two weeks after this conversation Ellen told Tom to sit down.

"What have I done wrong?" he said jokingly.

Ellen laughed.

"Nothing."

Ellen then told Tom that her ex-husband was selling off part of his business. He had a locksmiths business selling and cutting keys and attached to this he also has a security company which installed CCTV and burglar alarms. She told Tom her ex-husband's name was Garry and she had spoken to him with regards to what sort of money he wanted. She then told Tom that there was over two hundred thousand pounds of equity in her house and she could get enough of a mortgage to buy the business that Garry was selling.

"What do you think?"

Tom was taken aback and did not know what to say. Ellen could see his discomfort.

"Tom, from my point of view we are serious. Although we are not married I think of us as a permanent couple and you would not be doing this for yourself, it is our future."

Tom smiled.

"For me there is only us. If it's what you want, of course I would like it, but everything must be in your name. It is a stupid male pride thing."

The next day they both went to a Building Society to discuss the remortgaging and was assured that there was no problem. That afternoon they had made an appointment to see Garry.

At two thirty Ellen parked her car outside Garry's shop. Tom got out of the car just before Ellen and looked at the window. It was split in two with the door in the middle. On one side there were displayed various locks and keys and on the other side the window displayed cameras and detectors.

When they entered Garry was behind a counter with another man. He came round the counter and kissed Ellen on the cheek. He then turned to Tom and offered his hand for a handshake.

"Hello, Tom, nice to meet you. Follow me and we can go to my office at the back of the shop."

"Good to meet you too. I see we have similar taste in women."

All three of them laughed knowing that Ellen was the woman involved.

Both Tom and Ellen followed Garry to the back of the shop and through a door. In the middle of this room was a desk with one chair behind and two chairs in front. Garry took the single chair and Tom and Ellen sat opposite him.

Garry started the conversation.

"Has Ellen told you what this is about?"

"She told me you want to sell off part of the business, but I am ready to hear more."

Garry smiled and took a liking to Tom's directness. He continued.

"The plan is that I keep the locksmith side of the business and I was planning to sell the alarm and CCTV side. Is this of interest to you, Tom?"

Tom said it was.

Both men talked for the next hour and Ellen was pleased that her ex-husband and her new boyfriend got on so well. After the hour, Garry stopped and looked at Tom.

"I have another idea. Why don't you buy into a partnership in the whole business, I think we could work well together?"

Tom had taken a liking to Garry.

"I would be happy with that arrangement."

He turned to Ellen.

"What do you think?"

Ellen was so pleased with how this had all gone.

"I think that is a great idea. You two men don't only have good taste for women, you seem to get on well. Let's go for it."

Garry showed Tom the P and L (profit and loss) paperwork and the Balance Sheet. A sum of one hundred and ten thousand pounds was agreed and Garry said he would draw up the paperwork and they should be set to go within the next two weeks.

Tom had the pleasure of handing his notice in. JP was not disappointed and accepted Tom's resignation. Several months later Tom found out that JP had no real interest in the business and he sold the freehold making all of the staff redundant.

Tom joined Garry and for him, life was now perfect again. He and Ellen were great together and he got on so well with Garry. Most of their day was spent not only making money but having lots of fun along the way. They both had a similar sense of humour.

Garry enjoyed the locksmith side of the business and Tom took over the alarm and CCTV side. With the help of Lawrence who did the installation of the CCTV and the alarms, Tom soon learnt to do a survey of the house and where PIRs (passive infrared detectors) were best situated.

Tom had an enquiry from a company that supplied food for airplanes. He went to the City airport to meet the managing director. He found the name of the company and entered the reception of the offices. A young lady smiled as he entered and asked if she could help.

"I have an appointment to meet Mr. Grimes."

The young lady picked up the phone and said, "Mr. Grimes. Your two thirty appointment is here."

She nodded and told Tom to go down a passage and take the third door on the left.

Tom did as instructed and knocked lightly on the door. A voice from inside called out.

"Come in."

Tom entered the office and there was a man, probably in his late thirties, sitting behind a desk.

"Hello Mr. Levy," the man said. "Take a seat. My name is Barry Grimes and I am the managing director of the company."

Tom sat and replied, "Thank you for seeing me."

"We have premises in many airports around the world, but this one is new. The airport authorities insist on a certain amount of security due to us supplying planes directly with food and drink. I will take you down to the warehouse and you will tell me what is required. Is that okay?"

"That will be fine. You will have my recommendation within the next two days."

Tom followed Barry into the warehouse and Barry left him to look around. Tom, using one step as a one meter ruler, sketched out the layout of the warehouse. He was there for just over an hour. When Tom had finished he went back to the offices and told the receptionist that he was leaving and thanked her for her help.

When Tom got back to his own office he looked at his drawing of the warehouse. He thought, instead of writing down his recommendations, he could use his skills that he learned when designing salons. He had the cad program named 'Floor Plan' and using this and his approximate measurements he put the warehouse on his computer. He then added where cameras should go and show their viewing angles and also where PIRs should go. He spent three hours on this.

Late the next day Tom telephoned Barry to say he was ready to offer his proposals for their security. Barry told him to come in the following morning.

Tom was at the airport at nine in the morning and when he got to the reception he was told to go straight to Barry's office. Tom knocked quietly on Barry's door and Barry called out for him to come in.

"Good morning, Tom. What have you got for me?"

Tom said good morning and took out of his briefcase the drawing that he had done. He handed it to Barry.

He studied it for a little while and then said to Tom, "This is impressive. It makes my job easier as I have to get approval from the authorities and I can just give them this. Well done, Tom. Tell me about costs."

"For the complete job, including the computer and monitor, it will be just over twelve thousand pounds."

Barry stood up and held out his hand to be shaken.

"Let's do it. Start whenever you are ready."

Tom had been working with Garry for just over a year. Things were going well and Tom was pleased with how his life was working out.

One Wednesday evening after Tom and Ellen had finished eating Tom said, "Why don't we have a party?"

Ellen smiled and said, "Good plan. When should we do this?"

"After we are married," Tom said.

Ellen was stunned. She eventually said, "Are you serious?"

Tom went towards her and gave her a cuddle.

"If you want to, I want to."

The next few weeks were taken up with speaking to the rabbi and booking a date. Organising the party, hiring chairs and tables and booking a singer. The wedding was arranged for four weeks time.

On the day of the wedding there were eighty guests. Julien, Tom's son, came early and prepared the salmon, he had been a chef, and other members of the family helped with either preparing food or laying out the table around the swimming pool in their garden.

Tom and Ellen were married in a synagogue nearby. After the ceremony all of the guests went back to their house for the party.

The day was nice and sunny and everybody appeared to have a good time.

A major income for the business was the coming from monitoring the alarms. When customers bought an alarm system one of the options they had was to have their alarm system constantly monitored by a central station. For this they paid and annual sum to the business of two hundred pounds a year. Garry had amassed almost twelve hundred of these contracts over the years he had been in business. The only thing that the company had to do was to service each alarm system once a year. Each service took on average of ten to fifteen minutes so they had one engineer working solely on this.

After Tom had been with Garry for two years Garry had an offer from a national company who wanted to purchase these contracts. Their offer was a little less than two hundred thousand pounds. Tom and Garry together with Ellen sat down to discuss the offer.

The three of them sat round Garry's desk. Garry was first to speak.

"Well, what are your thoughts?"

Tom was first to reply.

"It is a difficult offer to refuse. The problem I see is that it will be difficult for the two of us to make a good living without these contracts."

Garry nodded.

"Well, if we sold the contracts you can buy me out." Ellen then spoke.

"It appears to me that this opportunity for all of us is too good to miss. I would be happy if we, Tom and myself, buy you out."

Garry looked at Tom.

"What do you think, Tom?"

"If Ellen is happy, I am happy."

Garry smiled.

"Okay, let's do this."

Garry handled the negotiations with the national company. After the deal was complete the three of them sat down again at Garry's table. Garry showed the accounts of the company and its value was three hundred and twenty thousand pounds meaning that it would cost either Garry or Tom one hundred and sixty thousand pounds to buy the other out.

The follow evening Ellen told Tom to sit down. He complied. She sat in the chair opposite him. She took a big breath.

"I have another idea and a reason to get Garry to buy us out."

Tom was a little shocked, but knew Ellen hadn't finished with her explanation.

"Tell me more."

Ellen was becoming more and more animated.

"I have seen a franchise for sale. It is a 'flood and fire' restoration company that works with insurance companies and we can afford it."

Tom was a little surprised but it was her house that started this project so he said, "If you think it is a good idea we shall go for it. Will you speak to Garry and find out if he wants to buy us out?"

She said she would and she would contact the business that was up for sale and arrange an appointment for them both.

Two days later Ellen told Tom that she had spoken to Garry and he was willing to buy them out. She had also made an appointment with the owner of the company for sale. The company was on an industrial estate just outside the town. They arrived on Friday evening and went into the unit. It was large with furniture lined up either side of the walls. There were stairs leading up to the offices. When they reached the top step they entered the office. It was long and there were three desks. On the final desk, furthest from the door, sat a man. He was probably in his forties. He stood up when they entered and Tom and Ellen went towards him. He offered his hand for shaking and the three of them shook hands.

"Hello, I am Raymond Thomas and this is my company," he said.

"Hello, my Name is Tom and this is Ellen, my wife."

Although Ellen was now his wife it came out naturally. All three of them sat down and Raymond took out some accounts for them to look at.

Looking at and understanding accounts was what Tom was used to from his time with the consultancy company. It appeared that the company got an average of sixty jobs a month from their Head Office. The figures looked good and it was making good profit.

"If you want you can take the accounts with you, but I will need them back at some time," Raymond said.

"Thank you. I will get these back to you by the day after tomorrow and I will have an answer for you then as to whether we proceed with the sale."

They all stood, shook hands again and Tom and Ellen left. The drive home was silent with both of then lost in their own thoughts.

"What do you think?" Ellen said when they got home

"The figures look good and when I value a business I expect to get my investment back within three to four years. Based on the figures I have seen, it looks possible."

Ellen then smiled.

"So, do we buy?"

"Yes," Tom responded.

Two days later Tom and Ellen went back to see Raymond. They handed his accounts back to him and said they would agree to the purchase of the business.

The sale took place two months later and Tom went to the business and met the staff. There were two technicians and a secretary. The older technician was named Trevor and the younger was named Paul. The secretary's name was Susan. Tom said hello to them all and they all went about their work. Susan helped Tom to understand the business.

She explained that their Head Office would designate a job to them. This could be a fire or flood that had made a claim to the insurance company. The insurance company would expect them to either put in de-humidifiers, if it was a flood, or arrange to clean the house if there was fire damage. The most profitable was fire because all of the clothes had to be specially cleaned to rid them of the smell of smoke.

After six months it all became easier but Tom noticed the instructions from Head Office appeared to be getting less and less. Head Office memos were constantly talking about 'self generated work', in other words, don't rely solely on work coming from insurance companies.

Tom went out looking for cleaning work, large factories, office blocks and anything similar. He attended business breakfast meeting twice a week and made as many contacts as he could. One day he was contacted by the manager of the town centre.

He was looking for a company to clean the streets in the town centre.

"Hello, my name is Malcolm Smith and I am the Town Centre manager. I am looking for a company that will clean the streets. Is this something you would be interested in?"

Tom said he would and made arrangements with Malcolm to go to his office the next day at ten o clock.

The next day Tom arrived at a large department store and went to the top floor where Malcolm's office was. On one of the glass doors Malcom's name was printed and Tom knock very gently on it. Malcolm called out to come in.

Tom entered a large office and Malcolm sat behind a large desk. Malcolm stood up and Tom joined him and both men shook hands.

"Hello, Mr. Smith, thank you for seeing me."

"Please call me Malcolm. Have a seat and we can discuss the project that I have."

Tom sat down. Malcolm explained that he wanted the street jet washed starting at four in the morning as the streets would be too busy later in the day.

"Is this something you would want to do?"

Tom's mind was racing. This was a huge opportunity, one not to be missed.

"Yes," he replied, "I cannot see a problem, but I will need two days to calculate the price for you. Can I come back to you on Friday to discuss this further?"

Malcolm said this would be fine and asked Tom, "Do you have time for a coffee? We can go to the restaurant downstairs."

"That sounds good," replied Tom, "I will pay and put it on your bill."

Both men laughed and Malcolm stood up ready to go.

They went down one set of stairs and into the restaurant and Malcolm told Tom to take a seat and he would bring the coffee to him.

Malcolm returned to the table with coffees. Conversation was easy, they had so much in common and they talked for just over two hours.

Tom left Malcolm at the restaurant and went back to his office to work out the logistic of jet washing the town centre. The first problem was carrying water, he would need either a small lorry or a Bowser. The next challenge would be to find staff to do this, starting at four in the morning and finishing at midday.

Later that afternoon when the technicians had returned from their job he called them into the office. Susan, the secretary, was already at her desk. He told them all about the town centre job and asked them if they knew anybody looking for work. Paul said his cousin was looking for work and he would speak to him tonight. Trevor, the other technician, said he may have somebody and he too would speak to them tonight.

After the other staff had gone home Tom stayed to work out the costs, labour, petrol, the cost of a second hand lorry etc. After nearly three hours Tom calculated the price to give to Malcolm would be just over ninety thousand pound a year. He had looked up the price of a second hand lorry and given this a three year write off. He could get a lorry for nine thousand pounds so he calculated this to cost three thousand pounds a year. He then went home to tell Ellen all about it.

The next morning Tom went to work early to recheck his calculations. When Paul arrived he was accompanied by two other people. One was a young man, Tom thought late teen or early twenties, and an older lady.

Paul said to Tom, "Good morning, Tom. This is my cousin John and his mother, Rita. They are interested in the town centre job."

Tom smiled and said, "Hi, Paul. Rita and John, please take a seat."

They both sat down in the chairs opposite Tom.

Tom explained to them what the job entailed and he discussed salary with them. They were both keen to have the job. Tom then explained that he would be visiting the Town Centre manager today to get confirmation of the job and he would need two weeks to get the equipment they would need. They all exchanged telephone numbers and Tom told them he would contact them as soon as he was ready to go.

Tom was now left in thought. According to the franchise agreement Tom would have to pay ten percent of all of his income to the franchise company. He already had two regular cleaning contracts, one was a pub and the other was a church. The income from these two was around ten thousand pounds a year which meant he had to pay the franchise company one thousand pounds a year. This was not too painful but, if he got the town centre job, his income from cleaning would be over one hundred thousand a year, ten thousand to the franchise company.

Tom resented the idea of this. It was him that found the work and the instructions from his Head Office had now dwindled to twenty a month, a far cry from when he bought the business of sixty a month. Tom made a decision to open another company and take his cleaning work away from his present business. Before he could do this he would have to speak to Malcolm to see if this effected their arrangement.

Tom telephoned Malcolm and arranged to go to Malcolm's office at lunchtime. Tom said, in good humour, that he would buy lunch. Malcom agreed and they were to meet on the restaurant.

Tom arrived at twelve o' clock and Malcolm was already seated. They ordered lunch and then Tom told Malcolm what the cost would be, but said he would need a two year contract. Tom needed this to at least cover his outlay. Malcolm said that this will be fine and he would draw up the contract. Tom then told Malcolm that he was making another company and he told him why.

Malcolm smiled and said, "I don't blame you. The leeches at your Head Office let you work and take their ten percent. I have no problem with whatever your business is called. Just tell me when you want to start."

"Thank you Malcolm, I will need a couple of weeks. Can I call you in a week and let you know?"

Malcolm laughed and said, "No. You can come and buy me lunch instead."

They both laughed.

When Tom got back to his office there was lots to do. He made a list for himself. Check if the lorry is still for sale. Look for companies that sold large water containers. Look for two powerful jet washes. Buy a 'pay as you go' phone to enable the team cleaning the streets to keep in touch with him.

He started with the lorry. It was still for sale and he went to have a look at it. It started well and Tom said he would buy it if he was given a three month warrantee for it. The seller agreed. Tom paid a deposit and said he would get it picked up early next week. They shook hands and Tom left.

When Tom got back to the office he asked his secretary, Susan, to look for companies that sold large water containers and also to find powerful jetwashers. By the end of the day Tom's list of 'things to do' was complete. He decided to buy Malcolm lunch next Wednesday to say he was almost ready to start, all that was needed was for Malcolm to supply him with a map of the town centre and for them to discuss where to start first.

Tom had spoken to Ellen and she was excited. She said that she would set up the new company and she would call it 'T and E Trading Limited'. Two days later, 'T and E Trading Limited' was alive. Tom contacted

John and Ruth and told them they would probably start on Monday a week. He said he would confirm with them after his meeting next Wednesday with Malcolm.

On the following Wednesday Tom met Malcolm in the restaurant and they had lunch mainly making social conversation. After lunch Tom went upstairs to Malcom's office and they studied the map. It was important to start the cleaning early on the busiest streets and they could do the back streets after nine in the morning. They agreed to start on Monday a week.

Tom telephoned John and told him where to collect the lorry. He then telephoned the seller of the lorry and told him who would collect it and they agreed to a money transfer for the outstanding amount. Tom told John to bring the lorry back to his office and he would go with him to buy the water containers and the jetwashes. Everything was going to plan.

John collected the lorry on the Thursday and Tom went with him to buy the rest of the equipment they would need. He gave John the phone and also the map of where they should start and told him they could start on Monday morning.

T and E Trading Limited, trading as Orbit Cleaning Services was born.

After two months everything was going well. Ellen had opened a second bank account and invoices to Malcolm, the pub and the church were sent with instructions to pay into this account. Tom had given Malcolm the number for John's phone so, if there was a problem, such as somebody had painted some graffiti on a wall, Malcolm could contact John to go and wash it off.

Tom now had time to look at the original business. Instructions were now down to twelve a month and Head Office saying that the insurance companies were 'cash settling' and not using restoration companies. Once the cleaning business was taken there was no way the business could survive. Tom decided to close it down.

He informed Head Office of his decision, they were not surprised, he was not the first, a number of other franchisees had already folded. Head Office told Tom that if he gave them a list of the equipment that he wanted to dispose of they would advertise it through the other franchisees. When it came closer to him actually closing down they would find another franchisee to take over his work in progress and they would settle with him when the jobs were complete.

Tom's next project was to try to find work for his two technicians and his secretary. He telephoned the nearest franchisees to see if they needed experienced staff. They said they did and asked Tom to send both the boys over to have a chat with the boss. Finding work for Susan was more difficult so he spoke to her and explained what was going to happen. She was not surprised and had expected it. She had also been looking for another job and she had already had two offers. Finally, Tom spoke to the landlord of the unit he rented and told him the problem. The landlord was sympathetic and said he would not hold him to the two outstanding years of his lease if he could rent it quickly.

The next year for Ellen and Tom was good. They were not rich but, with the help of Ellen's new hobby, making jewelry, which helped to subsidize their income, they lived well. They still managed to go to Egypt twice a year for their favorite pastime, snorkeling.

Ellen had become very artistic at making jewelry, mainly for women. Every weekend they went to a county fair and, when Tom got paid for the outstanding work, he bought a caravan so they could go further afield and stay the whole weekend. She did not make a fortune, sometimes six or seven hundred pounds, sometime they would just break even. Even when they just broke even they had a nice weekend.

Soon after two years, when Tom and Ellen were on one of their Egyptian holiday, Tom got a phone call from Robert who said he was the new manager of the Town Centre. Robert told him that Malcolm was no longer employed and he had made a decision to cancel the contract.

Tom did not want to tell Ellen as it would spoil their holiday and he spent the last few days keeping it secret. Ellen could feel something was wrong, but decided to let Tom tell her when he was ready. Tom was so angry with himself. How many managing directors had he told not to 'put all of their eggs in one basket' and to spread their client base to avoid exposure and here he was, losing ninety percent of his business through sheer stupidity.

On the flight home there was very little said. It was the same for the journey from the airport to their house. After Tom had taken the cases up to their bedroom he came down and sat at the kitchen table.

Ellen looked at him and poured two glasses of wine. She put one in front of Tom and she then sat on the chair opposite Tom. She put her hand towards Tom and he held it.

"Okay, its' time now to talk," she said. "What's wrong?"

Tom told her what a fool he had been and about the contract with the town centre. She listened without saying a word until he was finished speaking. She got up from the chair and went round the table and sat on Tom's lap. She then gently kissed him and said, "Don't worry, we will manage somehow. You still look good for an old man and I am sure we could still sell your body."

Tom smiled and realized he had been selfish to keep things quiet and to make her suffer. He kissed her and nodded.

"I don't think we shall get much from my body, but I am prepared to try."

She smiled and gave him a playful punch.

Tom felt better for telling her and the evening was pleasant.

Chapter 18

The next morning Tom telephoned his friend Kevin. Kevin owned a property management company. He looked after rented properties on behalf of the owners and made sure that the rents were paid and he also took care of any repairs that the house might need. Tom asked Kevin if he had a few minutes to spare and Kevin told him to come to his office whenever he wanted to. Tom said he would be there midday.

The drive to Kevin's office was less than ten minutes and Tom parked in one of the spaces that Kevin used for clients and staff. He then entered the office and said hello to the staff in the first office and he walked into Kevin's office.

After the handshakes and hellos Tom told Kevin what had happened.

"If you know or hear of anybody wanting cleaning can you let me know, please."

Kevin thought for a moment.

"I can't think of anybody off hand but I will let you know if I hear anything. What are you going to do, Tom?"

Tom shrugged his shoulders.

"I really do not know at the moment."

"I don't know if this will interest you but I need somebody to do two days marketing for me here. I am paying one hundred pounds a day. Interested?"

Tom smiled and said, "Yes, very much."

They agreed that Tom would come in to the office on Tuesdays and Thursdays, then Tom left, thanking Kevin one again.

When Tom got home he told Ellen about his conversation with Kevin. She was delighted for him, he needed an ego boost.

"That's eight hundred pounds a month from Kevin, Orbit cleaning earns almost two hundred pounds and we probably make between six and eight hundred pounds from the jewelry. That's sixteen hundred pounds a month, minimum. We can survive."

She smiled and Tom smiled back.

On the following Tuesday Tom arrived at the office. Kevin had prepared a desk for him and he asked Tom to telephone their clients to find out if they were satisfied and generally do public relations on them. This was Tom's task for now, but eventually he would have to find ways to get more landlords on the books.

Tom still spoke to Maurice at least once a week and occasionally met him for lunch. Maurice was well into his eighties and had told Tom he was getting tired. Tom knew Maurice had more than forty properties of his own and suggested to Maurice that he met with Kevin. Maurice agreed and Tom set up the meeting for the following week.

Maurice and Kevin got on very well and Maurice instructed Kevin to manage his properties. They agreed on a reduced commission as there were forty one properties. Tom felt good as he had repaid Kevin's kindness. The situation went on for a couple of months with Tom and Ellen doing a craft show every weekend.

Tom worked hard at whatever he was doing but he always had the feeling that Kevin was being charitable.

One evening when Tom got home from the office Ellen made him sit at the kitchen table. When he was sat she brought her laptop to the table and put it in front of him. Tom looked at the screen and being advertised was a beachside house in Spain being sold for one hundred and thirty thousand Euros.

Tom looked at Ellen.

"Why are you showing me this?"

"I have been doing some thinking and some sums. If we didn't have a mortgage we could probably live on two to three hundred pounds a week. There is just over three hundred thousand pounds of equity in this property which means I can give my girls fifty thousand pounds each and we would be able to buy something like this with cash, no mortgage. Two to three markets a week and I think we could live well. What do you think?"

Tom was stunned. He looked at Ellen and said. "Are you serious?"

"Yes," she said. "What do you think?"

Tom thought for a little while. The idea of not feeling that Kevin was being charitable, the idea of living by the sea somewhere warm and the thought that this June he would get his pension seemed to be great.

"I cannot think of a negative at the moment," he replied. "It does sound like a good idea."

Ellen got up and poured two glasses of wine. She handed one to Tom and lifted her glass up to offer a toast.

"Here's to the future," she said.

They chinked their glasses.

That night was spent making plans of how this was to be done. They agreed that it would take three months to sell the house so the one they had looked at would probably have been sold by then so it was unanimously agreed that they would rent a property in an area that was touristy which would be a better market for the jewelry. Then, when the opportunity to buy something came, they would have the money to pay cash.

The next day Ellen contacted some estate agents to ask about their commission rates and she made appointment with three of them to come to the house to offer their suggestions of what the asking price should be. She chose one because she liked the agent and also he thought he could get the best price. The house was now up for sale.

Within three weeks they had an offer on the house which they accepted and all that was left to do was the legalities. Ellen put her car up for sale as they agreed that they would use Tom's car to drive to Spain. They studied maps of Spain and decided to move to Mallorca.

Because the house was in Ellen's name they both decided that Tom would drive there and find a property to rent and Ellen would fly there and join him once the house purchase was complete.

Three months after Ellen came up with this scheme Tom loaded his car and set off to drive to Mallorca. The journey would take approximately twenty three hours so Tom decided to do it in three days, roughly eight hours driving a day. He had already planned the route and booked hotels where he would stop for the night.

When Tom arrived in Mallorca it was early evening on a Friday. He looked for an inexpensive hotel that would be his base until he found a property to rent. He booked a room and then went out for something to eat. By nine thirty he was in bed, exhausted.

Mallorca, being a tourist hotspot, sold everything English, including a local newspaper that was printed in English. Tom bought one of these the next morning after he had breakfast. On the back page there were a number of properties for rent. Tom saw three that he liked and made appointments to view them.

The first two he saw were okay but he didn't feel were right for them. The third one, which was the most expensive, was on the beach and looked similar to the one that Ellen had shown him three months ago. The rent was three hundred and fifty Euros a month and Tom told the owner that he would take it. He paid the owner seven hundred Euros, one month's rent in advance and one month's rent as a deposit. He telephoned Ellen that night and told her about their next place they will live in. She was really happy.

Tom spent the next three weeks finding out where things were. He discovered three local markets and spoke to the men who ran them and asked what the situation was to rent a stall. He wrote all of this down for when Ellen would come to join him. He then walked around the town to look for suppliers of gemstones for Ellen. There were three shops which would probably do.

Two weeks later Tom drove to the airport to collect Ellen. He saw her coming out of 'arrivals' and they both could not wait for their first cuddle for weeks. Tom took her case and showed her where the car was parked and they then drove to their new home, talking non-stop.

When they arrived at the beach house Ellen was like an excited child, jumping up and down and clapping her hands together. Tom had prepared food the night before so, by the time Ellen had unpacked, Tom had the food on the table. They ate and drank a whole bottle of wine that night.

The next three weeks were spent going to the markets and booking a 'pitch', visiting the shops that Tom had found, to get Ellen's stock full, and visiting a bank so that both of them could open an account. Tom had to contact the Pension Office to tell them about his change of address and also his new bank account. He was told that money would be paid into this account every four weeks and told that this would be paid in Euros and would be the equivalent of roughly eight hundred pounds depending on the exchange rate.

This was not yet the peak tourist season, but the three markets were earning them roughly four hundred Euros a week and, together with Tom's pension, they were making in excess of two thousand Euros a month. They did the same in these markets as they used to in the craft fairs, Tom serving and Ellen making. It always amused Ellen how much Tom flirted with the ladies but she always knew who he was going home with. Her.

After they had been there for six weeks they met another couple of similar age who had retired there. They all got on well and as well as dinner parties, they had card evenings, and Bob, whose full name was Bob Moreland, taught Tom and Ellen to play Mahjong. Bob's wife was named Rita. This had to be on the nights there were no markets because the markets started at two in the afternoon and went on till eleven in the evening, sometimes till midnight.

One evening, when Tom and Ellen arrived at Bob and Rita's house there was another couple there. Bob introduced them.

"Hello, Tom and Ellen, this is George and Lisa Wright. This is Tom and Ellen Levy."

They all shook hands. George and Lisa had also come to the island after George retired and it transpired that they live just one hundred meters along the coast for Tom and Ellen. Bob had made food for everyone and Tom had bought a couple of bottles of wine.

The six of them became inseparable and spent a lot of time together. Lisa said to Ellen that there was a house three doors from their place that was up for sale. This was the one thing that did not make their life perfect, she wanted their own house. She arranged to meet Lisa the next day to have a look at the house.

The next day Ellen walked to Lisa's house and Lisa made coffee.

"Come on, I will show you the house," Lisa said. "I have already spoken to the owners and they have given me the keys, they are away for a couple of day."

Ellen followed Lisa and they walked past two beachside houses and came to the one that was for sale.

Ellen could not stop laughing. Lisa was confused.

"What is so funny?"

Ellen stopped laughing and said, "This house is the reason we are here."

She went on to tell Lisa how she showed this house to Tom and that is what started them on this journey.

"It is fate," Ellen said. "We have to buy this house."

Lisa told Ellen it was up for sale at one hundred and thirty five thousand Euros, but she thought the owners would take an offer. Ellen thanked Lisa and asked her if she could contact the owners and ask what their bottom price was. Lisa said she would. Ellen then walked home and couldn't wait to tell Tom.

Tom and Ellen bought the house two weeks later for the sum of one hundred and thirty thousand Euro, the same price they saw it for a long time ago. They moved into the house four weeks later and had a house warming party with Bob, Rita, George and Lisa.

Three weeks later Ellen was preparing breakfast, she had left Tom in bed. It was now eleven o clock and Ellen started to worry. Tom never slept beyond nine thirty.

She went upstairs to the bedroom intending to call him 'lazy', but when she walked into the room she saw Tom sweating. His face was flushed and his breathing was labored. She went to him and touched his forehead. It was burning. She ran downstairs and called a doctor she knew. He said he would be there in ten minutes.

Eight minutes later the doctor arrived. He examined Tom and said he had pneumonia. He told Ellen he would give Tom an injection now but she must get the medicine he prescribed as soon as possible. He also told Ellen to try to give Tom as much water as possible. He injected Tom and said, "I am not sure we should hospitalize him, but I will come back tomorrow and see how he is."

Ellen thanked him and he left.

Ellen didn't want to leave Tom so, although Lisa was only three houses away, she telephoned her and told her about Tom. Lisa said she would come straight away.

Lisa arrived within the minute. She went upstairs to see Tom.

"You stay here with Tom," she then said to Ellen. "I will go and get the medicine. Keep a cold towel on him and try to give him as much water as possible. Now, give me the prescription and I will go to the pharmacy."

Ellen handed the prescription to Lisa and went downstairs to get more water.

The doctor came the next day and said that there had been an improvement, probably due to the injection. He injected Tom once more and said he would come back the next day.

The same process went on for the next week and Tom's fever had broken, he was starting to speak and even drank some soup. Two weeks later Tom managed to get out of bed and slowly walked downstairs.

Four weeks after Tom was diagnosed with pneumonia Tom and Ellen started to take short walks along the beach. Every day they increased the amount of time they walked.

Tom, through his illness, had lost a lot of weight so walking was slow. On the fifth week after being ill both Tom and Ellen walked along the sand. They were saying how perfect their life had turned out and how happy they were.

When they got back to their house Tom kissed Ellen and said, "I am going to sit on our patio for a bit and watch the sea."

Ellen said she was going in to have a shower and she would join him with the wine soon. They both smiled at each other.

Twenty minutes later Ellen arrived at the patio. Tom had his eyes closed. She looked at him and it seemed like he was smiling in his sleep. She silently crept up to him and tenderly kissed him on his lips. Tom didn't react.

"Tom," she whispered.

He still didn't react. She then gently shook his shoulder. Tom still didn't move. She shook him more violently. He still didn't move.

Tears welled up in her eyes and then she convulsed with sobs. She knew it wasn't a deep sleep, it was a forever sleep.

The End

Author's Note:

If you enjoyed this book people have said that they enjoyed the 'follow up' book even more. It is titled, "My life after Tom"